# Vanished in the Dunes

# Vanished in the Dunes

## A Hamptons Mystery

Allan Retzky



Oceanview Publishing
Longboat Key, Florida

FIRST EDITION



This book is a work of fiction. Names, characters, businesses, organizations, places, and incidents either are the products of the author's imagination or are used fictitiously. Any resemblance to actual events, businesses, locales, or persons, living or dead, is entirely coincidental.

ISBN: 978-1-60809-053-2

Published in the United States of America by Oceanview Publishing,
Longboat Key, Florida
www.oceanviewpub.com

2 4 6 8 10 9 7 5 3 1

PRINTED IN THE UNITED STATES OF AMERICA

For Susan

# ACKNOWLEDGMENTS

When an international commodity trader transitions to fiction writing, there are many to thank for their support and input. I gratefully salute those whose assistance made this work possible.

A toe in the water at The Writers Studio in Manhattan afforded me some initial confidence, thanks to the tolerance and skills of Lesley Dorman and Cynthia Weiner.

The Southampton College Graduate Writing Program, under the remarkable leadership of Robert Reeves, provided the groundwork for my writing. The extraordinary faculty was always there to teach and encourage. My work benefited in particular from the intellectual and teaching skills of Clark Blaise, Ursula Hegi, Kaylie Jones, Matt Klam, Bharti Mukherjee, and Lou Ann Walker.

This novel had its own specific need for expertise. Detective Peter Schmidt of the East Hampton Police Department professionally described local law enforcement activities; I apologize if my liberal use of literary license transformed the department's procedures into something less recognizable. Dr. Robert Sussman led me through the scope of mental illnesses and the range of effects from various medications. Any errors of fact are completely my own.

My agent, Ellen Levine of Trident Media, never lost faith in the novel and her constructive suggestions reshaped the story's focus and propelled it forward. And special thanks to the editorial skills of Dr. Patricia Gussin of Oceanview Publishing who believed in the book from the onset. My thanks to the Oceanview team, Bob Gussin, Frank Troncale, David Ivester, Susan Hayes, and George Foster.

Thanks also to an array of colleagues and friends who were unstinting in their reinforcement of my efforts. You all showed remarkable patience.

My final appreciation goes to the most important requisite element, my primary support group—my family. Andrea Retzky, and Deborah, Bob, Anna, and Daniel Shaul offered constructive criticism and relentless encouragement. Most of all, my wife and best friend, Susan, supported my efforts from the very beginning, always willing to read, take a breath, and then reread some more. None of this would have happened without her.

Amagansett, New York
January 2012

# Vanished in the Dunes

# CHAPTER 1

Posner first sees the woman in profile as she moves past him at the bus stop. There is a flash of a pink-and-white dress, smooth tanned arms, and black hair cut short with a tight curl that kisses her ears. He doesn't know why he looks up at that moment. Perhaps it is just habit, seeing if the bus has turned the corner, or possibly it's the flicker of her dress's pink that seizes the edge of his eye, but as soon as she passes, he returns to his newspaper.

He's waiting for the Hampton Jitney to take him to Amagansett on the East End of Long Island. But for Amos Posner, the summer season, which officially begins in four weeks with the Memorial Day weekend, brings too many people, too much noise, an excess of money and boasts, all of which he has been trying to avoid for the last two years.

He waits in front of a Victoria's Secret window on 86th Street. The bus is due at 8:30 a.m., but it is already a few minutes late. He folds the *New York Times* in half and slides it into the backpack between his legs. A few years ago he carried a wide expandable leather briefcase, but circumstances have drastically changed his life, and he finds the backpack roomier and more convenient. The air is cool and spasms of wind appear and vanish with indecisive regularity. The beach will be much cooler than the city. He knows this from years of irregular residence in Amagansett.

The woman stops a few yards away and again draws the corner of his vision as she looks up at the Jitney sign. She has no suitcase, but carries a large straw bag. She speaks to a man standing nearby, who, pointing to the bus sign, seems to confirm that she is standing in the right place. Posner briefly studies her face, olive complexioned like his own, a nose with a small bump in its center, a full-lipped mouth. Silver hoop earrings contrast with her dark skin. The dress fits a bit too tightly around her body and the skirt seems shorter than is stylish. She has nothing of his wife Sara's classic good looks or elegance, yet the woman emits an effortless erotic aura.

The bus pulls to a stop at the curb just as Posner moves to the spot where he knows the door will open. A solitary newspaper page races determinedly through the morning air just past where he stands, as if it, too, wishes to board and escape the city. The paper plunges to a stop as it clings to a post that carries a parking sign, before it gently slides down to the sidewalk. That's as far as you'll go today, Posner muses as he turns toward the just-opened door.

The woman is presumably somewhere behind him now, waiting with the few who will board at this first pickup spot. Posner knows the driver and attendant—regulars on this run, as is he. Nevertheless, he calls out, "Amagansett," and moves up the stairs. He finds an aisle seat a bit more than halfway down and drops his backpack on the adjoining window seat. He removes his newspaper from the backpack, leans into the seat, and stifles a yawn.

Pulling out the Wednesday sports section, he begins to scan the headlines just as a flicker of pink and white passes and moves farther toward the rear. He briefly follows the movement until she passes, then contemplates her circumstances, as if it were a kind of challenge, like the old television show, *What's My Line?* where a celebrity panel must ponder the occupation of a mystery guest. Posner guesses that her occupation is that of a housekeeper or nanny, and that she has been in the city for a night to visit family or friends. Her features and coloring lead him to believe she has probably emigrated from some place far more exotic than the Hamptons. Satisfied that he has solved the origin and occupation options of the young woman, he looks in earnest at the review of a Yankee victory the previous night.

The bus picks up more passengers on 59th Street, but the majority of commuters will enter on 40th Street. That's where he drops the paper in his lap and looks up to see if he will need to relinquish the seat where his backpack rests. He studies the passengers. At this early hour, the young males usually opt for the very rear, where they are likely to find a double seat to spread their bodies out and sleep. The occasional men in suits are likely day-trippers who have some business meeting worthy of the more than four-hour, two-way commute. They congregate toward the front, folding their jackets neatly and resting them in the overhead bin, as if they were fragile antiques. Young women often seek each other out, grasping cups of coffee from the store at the bus stop.

In a few minutes Posner is satisfied that the seat next to him will remain empty. He scans the business section. Just as the bus enters the Midtown Tunnel, he is drawn to an article under the fold. The headline shouts the news of the indictment of a financial executive for bribing foreign officials. He feels a chill dance across his back and his pulse rate elevates. He has felt this way before, but not in a few years. He believed all of this was behind him. He forces himself to read through the article. He does not know the man, but the transaction description is all too familiar.

For two years he has waited for a call from the Justice Department. In his address book he keeps the name and number of a lawyer, a specialist in challenging government accusations of misconduct in such matters. He waits in limbo for a call that may never come while the statute of limitations runs toward expiration.

He knows the Justice Department is still involved and has not yet decided to dismiss the case. The authorities have in recent years showed a particular interest in transactions that involve excessive payments to foreign agents to secure overseas business in a country where honest auctions are unknown. If he had worked for a public company, the Securities and Exchange Commission might also have tracked the matter, but his past employer was a private, family-owned business, so there is no question of securities fraud, but this is small consolation. He has lived with this issue without comfort. The smallest thing can set him off into an orbit of worry that might take days to ease. His mind tells him that he is innocent, at most a dupe of more senior people's ambitions, but he sees no easy resolution.

He folds the business section and stuffs it in the mesh pocket of the seat in front, as if this gesture will make the story disappear. He takes deep breaths and turns toward the window. The face in the return image has been called nice looking. When they were first married, Sara even teasingly described his looks as a small step below really handsome, but he was never comfortable with that assessment. He is a bit less than six feet with all his dark hair still in place. His eyes are brown, yet there is weariness in his reflection he can't hide from himself or others.

They leave the tunnel and are on the expressway. An attendant offers muffins and juice, but he waves her off. His stomach has a hollow void that food will not fill. He stares out the window until his eyes flutter closed.

His nap is short lived as the attendant provides the ritual announcement regarding fares. Posner slips his discount coupon from his wallet and wedges it into the back of the broken tray table. He has already printed his name and destination, so the attendant will not bother him with personal details for the computer database, but the interruption has voided any further possibility of sleep. He pulls his wrist up and checks the time. Traffic must be light. They are already past the Great Neck exit. Less than two hours to go.

A cluster of dark clouds moving east parallels the bus. He cannot shake this new angst. Two years have passed since his last attack of fear, but nothing has been resolved: not today's paper's veiled dark portent about the Foreign Corrupt Practices Act, nor how he might be personally involved. He has been forced to resign, but the owners attempted to make it appear as amicable as possible. His severance was generous, yet there was an agreement provision that the same severance would be forfeited to the extent of full recapture if he provided any evidence of past irregularities to authorities. The agreement is probably unenforceable, according to Sara, a lawyer, as well as the special attorney he consulted, but he still signed it. He is now basically unemployable at fifty-five. At least he has the house near the beach he tells himself, the mortgage all paid off, and the isolation from commercial matters, a small consolation.

Sara continues to work in mergers for a medium-sized law firm where she recently became a partner. That's why they keep the one-bedroom apartment on East 90th Street. She left a note on the kitchen table this morning saying she may arrive at the beach late in the evening since she is driving to a meeting on the East End of Long Island. She asked if he could pick her up at the entrance to the East Hampton Airport terminal around nine after she drops off the rental car. Her plan to come out to the beach is a welcome idea, but he's not sure if she'll actually show up since they've barely spoken over the past several weeks.

Their marriage has been in a downward spiral for some time now. Sara was originally sympathetic to his potential legal problem, and she freely enjoys the revenue derived from his earlier success. More recently, she seems disinterested in his legal concerns and focuses more on his diminishing interest in sex. She hasn't bought into the explanation that the stress of his legal problems coupled with his job loss has upset his libido despite such confirmation by a urologist. At first, he hoped that she would come to understand, but as he retreated further into his world at the beach she had another theory.

It came to a head six weeks ago on a Sunday at the beach house as she was getting ready to return to New York. There would soon be a ride back with a neighbor. She stood across from him in the living room her legs straddling the small weekend bag stuffed with the laptop and the usual selection of work files she always brought with her.

"I need to know if you're seeing someone else. Someone local. Is that why you always want to be here? Do you want someone younger? Someone available on a moment's notice?"

"There's no one else. I swear."

She started to walk down the steps, then stopped halfway down, turned, and faced him.

"I just don't know if I can believe you."

And she hasn't spent a night at the beach since that Sunday. Oh, he'd spent time in the city since then, but it wasn't the same as it had once been. When he was in town, she was so distant as to make him feel isolated in his own apartment even though he thought spending more time in the city would defuse her accusations.

Then there was this morning's surprise note that she might make it out to the beach for the night and take a bus back later the next day. After reading today's newspaper story, a part of him would prefer if she didn't come today. Still, if it means she wants to be with him, then it'll be well worth it. Maybe today will be different. If she does come out we'll do something special. Something to pull him out of his funk over the foreign bribery mess and maybe begin to repair things between them. A quiet dinner tomorrow in the garden room at the American Hotel would work. He makes a mental note to book a table and sips from the small complimentary water bottle the attendant distributed during the first minutes of the trip.

He looks up as the bus turns off the expressway at the Manorville exit. He notices that the dark cloud has turned even blacker and continues to follow their route, as if waiting to be united with the bus at some distant point. Posner shivers slightly, then aggressively turns pages as he searches for the crossword puzzle. Indiscriminate words hold no fear for him. He works on the puzzle intermittently as the bus makes its ritual stops in Southampton and other small villages.

"Excuse me, but is the East Hampton beach near the bus stop?"

The voice comes from just behind him. He turns. The pink-and-white dress has moved from some seat in the back and now stands in the aisle. One arm stretches above to hold the railing under the storage bins. The pose is almost erotic in its effect. The pitch of the voice is low and throaty. He detects some accent, something European. Somehow he thinks of rushing water. He gathers himself into speech.

"It's not too close. You can get a taxi to take you there, but the weather doesn't look too promising for the beach."

He might have said that he wasn't sure, or something equally evasive, but the simple act of engaging this woman in conversation, has an immediate effect on his anguish, which he feels slipping away. He has an almost unnatural motivation to keep the conversation alive.

"How come you're out here on such a cool day if you want to see the beach?" he asks.

The bus nears the turn to East Hampton; there are but a few minutes left before it stops.

"I just wanted to see the beach. Ever since I'm in New York, I've heard how beautiful the beaches are. I have the day off, so I thought I'd have a look."

"A day off from what?" he asks, as he wonders about his first assessment. The woman raises both arms and smoothes her hair, as if posing. The motion propels her chest forward. He feels the hair on the back of his neck stand up, as if he's just entered a cold room.

"I'm a resident in psychiatry at Mt. Sinai. Wednesday is my day off," she answers in the matter-of-fact way people describe the most mundane things, like what car they own, or the movie they saw the past weekend.

This simple disclosure catches Posner unawares. So much for initial judgments, he thinks, but he recovers quickly enough to ask about her accent.

"*Ach*. That is German. I grew up in Austria, in Vienna. That's after my parents left Iran just before the shah and his family did."

Everything is clear now to Posner, the facial coloring and the accent all come together. And a doctor, no less. She must have sensed his surprise. She's probably seen it many times, but before he can say a word the bus begins to slow as it approaches the East Hampton stop. The empty driveway of the Palm Restaurant lies to the right. She stands and moves a step closer up the aisle and stops next to where he sits. The movement causes her to sway slightly and her hip brushes his shoulder. She seizes his eyes with her own, a pair of wide black bullets that bore through him, a discomfort he cannot evade.

"Do you get off here?" she asks, still swaying slightly as the bus slows. "Perhaps you can drop me at the beach."

"Sorry, but I go on till Amagansett," he answers. "Next stop."

She nods slightly. "Too bad." Her eyes remain locked on his.

The bus stops. "Well, thank you anyway," she says, and offers her hand.

It all seems very formal to Posner. Very European. Her grip is warm, and he senses her fingers linger across his palm far longer than normal. But what is normal?

"Enjoy," he says and releases her hand. He watches her walk down the aisle, briefly wonders why she was flirting with him, and smiles at the idea. The woman is probably only slightly more than half his age. Whatever it is, he feels a physical quiver where he has become used to near dormancy.

As the bus pulls away, he catches a flicker of pink and white against green foliage as she heads in the direction of the village shops. In a moment the bus escapes the area and he awaits the five-minute drive into Amagansett. The woman diverts his attention from his legal issues for a few minutes, but as soon as she leaves, his angst resurfaces with even greater intensity. He concentrates on a relaxation exercise where he breathes in and out slowly. It always seems to help.

A few minutes later, the bus slows and the gasp from the air brakes shakes him back to reality. He is the last passenger. He begins the short walk to the parking lot behind the library.

He finds the car, a new blue Lexus, hiding where he'd left it two days ago. Sara bought the car for cash from her own account the previous October. Since he lost his job and his severance has nearly disappeared, she now pays for everything. The Lexus was her choice although he would have preferred a more modest car, a hybrid, but he had no input.

"She's the one who's ringing the cash register now," her colleague Howard had said at the reception he attended a few months before that celebrated her law firm's twenty-fifth anniversary. Howard had been more than a little drunk when he spoke, but everything he said was true, however impolitic.

He sits motionless in the front seat, staring at the empty stretch of field beyond the parking lot. Tiny green shoots dot the earth. Regeneration, he thinks, but not for him. He is essentially unemployable within the international trading community, although there has been no publicized accounting of his activities. There is, however, a unique form of radar that links all elements in the relatively small commercial sector that deals in commodities. For millennia, the stock in trade for those whose survival depended on sound trading was clear and accurate information. Adverse weather, strikes, revolutions, mechanical failures all shaped supply and demand. Posner himself had once singularly procured information about the unanticipated early arrival of a large cargo of aluminum metal into Rotterdam at a time of great shortage. The cargo would replenish depleted stocks and prices would decline, but not before Posner sold considerable quantities short. He had acquired the correct information at the cost of a modest bribe to the ship owner's agent for daily updates on its arrival expectations.

But now he is little more than damaged goods. The same intelligence network that affords traders the opportunity to grasp early options now exposes the potential dangers in employing someone who might lead authorities to their door.

He has considered other employment options, but Wall Street is no longer one of them, the rejections were too long to list. He had always wanted to be an architect, ever since his parents took him to an Art Deco museum show. In high school he would endlessly design buildings, based on the ideas in that show. He wanted to build houses with new, spacious interiors. He wanted to renovate every aging brownstone in New York into airy, sun-filled homes. He wanted to do all this and his father, Stephen Posner, grandson of immigrant refugees from the Kishinev pogrom, agreed with enthusiasm.

"He will help build a better America," his father said a few months before his first year of Cornell's five-year architecture program. "We will find the money."

And somehow the money was there, at least for his first two years. Then there was his father's heart attack. He sat in a class that discussed how to measure stresses on structures when an aide brought a message to the teacher who interrupted the lecture to call him forward. His father was ill and his family wanted him to go home as soon as possible. His father had already died, but he wouldn't know that for seven hours. That's how long it took to take the bus from Ithaca to New York City, and then the subway ride and bus trip to the Bayside, Queens, house that was the only home he'd ever known. He never returned to Cornell. There was no money, and they needed money. His mother's brother had a Wall Street job and arranged for an interview with a firm that needed a trainee for their commodities group. He got the job and never left the industry. The only remnant of his architectural interest was a framed preliminary sketch he made years before of the house he now lives in.

He inserts the key into the ignition. The car still smells of new leather. Even if this is the car Sara wanted, he has the satisfaction of driving it to the home he chose and paid for out of his own earnings nearly twenty years ago, even before he and Sara had ever met. He takes considerable pleasure in this recollection.

The house is modern and sits on nearly half an acre of high dune only a block from the beach. A gray crushed-stone driveway climbs from the street amidst thick sand pines. A red quarry tiled entrance floor leads to four bedrooms and two baths, and a steep flight of wooden stairs just beyond the front door provides access to the main living quarters, a master bedroom suite, kitchen, and open living and dining areas. The exterior upstairs walls are interspersed with large floor-to-ceiling windows. There are wraparound decks and dramatic views of the ocean.

There is also a desk and chair from which he enjoys these views, a place where he now writes a history of his indiscretions. He often wonders if that is the correct word, but the meaning is clear, if only to him. He writes about his days in Iran, Venezuela, Chile, and Japan, and the bribes he's paid to obtain contracts. He remembers the envelopes he's passed over cocktails, the nods and winks that preceded every transaction, each the understated language of modern business, the lingua franca of twentieth-century corruption, although the practice has been entrenched for thousands of years.

"What will it take to make this business work?" he asked the ultimate buyer or seller, in words that have been repeated for centuries. Nothing has changed, except that penalties for such activities now exist. So he writes about what he has done. He does not think of this manuscript as a form of memoir. It is more or less a confessional of sorts. The process of writing eases his guilt, although the painful risk of discovery remains. His prose justifies his innocence. He only obeyed his senior managers. He didn't realize such activities were illegal. His justifications rise to absurd heights. His efforts helped an underdeveloped country obtain needed foreign currency, or have, in the national interest, profited American companies at the expense of overseas competitors.

He was fired shortly after the first Justice Department query letter arrived two years ago. With little else to do, he began writing. Writing the truth was all he has left. The company CEO remains. Yearly Christmas cards arrive, a smiling family portrait fronting a fireplace. He wonders why the CEO seems so secure while he is tormented. But he was the fall guy. The CEO's smile says: "Tough shit, Posner."

A car horn returns Posner to the present. He moves out of the lot past the library until a delivery truck blocks the exit. He wants to get home and return to his writing, but he realizes he should pick up a few food items for Sara. If she comes as promised, she'll arrive too late for anything more than something light to eat. The delay lasts a few minutes and his mind wanders. When the traffic finally moves, he swings his car to the right toward East Hampton.

He stops at the Suffolk County National Bank's drive-by ATM. The last CD from his working days has just matured. It's money he's earned and saved before he lost his job. He withdraws five hundred dollars. Now he won't need to touch the joint account for some time and a renewed feeling of even temporary financial independence quickens his pulse.

He pushes the Lexus to maximum legal speed until he enters a slow lane of traffic. He finally nears the corner of Newtown Lane and Main Street, the village's only major commercial intersection, and is surprised to see two empty spots in front of Citarella's, the newest upscale food emporium. He executes a U-turn at the Chase Bank and effortlessly swings the Lexus eastbound. At that moment he almost wants to thank Sara for the car's mobility. He approaches the corner where the Citarella store sits, but in less than a minute the spots are already taken, so he pulls into the rear lot.

He collects a pound of cooked shrimp, a few ripe tomatoes, a wedge of Gruyère, and a sourdough baguette. All these are Sara's favorites and should please her, although at this point he feels unsure whether it's likely to warm the atmosphere. It's just as possible she'll say a late lunch has diminished her appetite. He's about to head to the checkout when he decides to pick up lunch. At the take-out section, he selects the first sandwich he sees in the bin. He is not a picky eater. He chooses chicken and avocado. He could have done worse, he thinks, as he plucks a Diet Sprite and moves to the cashier.

He sits at one of the outside stone tables despite the chill. He is suddenly very hungry. His last meal was a chef's salad the previous night at a local Manhattan bistro.

"Oh, so it's you."

The words draw his eyes upward. The woman in pink and white stands above him, a burst of white teeth against tanned skin. He has never gotten used to people who smile so openly.

"May I join you?" she asks, resting a hand on the back of the other seat even before he can answer. Such tables are meant for sharing, yet she wants to be invited, and so he waves his hand while his wiry five-foot eleven body swivels to the side to let her pass.

This is the first opportunity to see her face without turning his neck. Her skin is remarkably smooth, as if she is newborn, her natural pink lips full to bursting. There is eye makeup and her brows are neat and dark, but he sees no other artificiality. He hesitates for words. He has rarely engaged a woman like this, but it is all frivolous and Sara is, frankly, not here to think otherwise. He suddenly enjoys the opportunity to relax.

“I thought you got off at a later stop,” she says.

“I did, but I needed to shop,” he answers and pulls the shopping bag upward.

She ignores his bag, saying, “Can you show me the beach?” She is almost so direct that he nearly winces.

All he can think to say is, “If you want to see the beach, you can take a taxi, or I guess I can drop you there.”

“That’s good,” she says without hesitation, yet even before the last words leave his mouth he realizes that a line has been crossed. He has left an opening, and a part of him, that piece of brain housing genetic material that determines conscience, hopes she declines. He has never been unfaithful to his wife, nor even considered it, despite Sara’s recent illusions. Yet this woman whom he now admits to himself looks exotically attractive does nothing to dispel this thought as she accepts the invitation.

“That sounds great.” She reiterates her approval. “Thank you.”

She replaces the top on her soup container and carefully lowers it together with the plastic spoon, wedge of bread, and napkin into a bag that matches his. He stands and directs her to the rear lot and into his car.

“It’s chilly here,” she says from the bench at the very back of the beach, only steps from where he parked. He has taken her to Atlantic Avenue Beach in Amagansett. There are no other cars, the unseasonable cool keeps everyone away save a couple dressed in yellow rain slickers standing near the water, tossing shells into the breakers.

She holds her cup of soup, which she says is too spicy, but nevertheless she eats greedily. In the short drive from where they met, introductions are exchanged. Her name is Heidi Kashani.

“I know Heidi is not a common American name,” she says, “but it is very normal in Austria.”

He agrees and tells her that he likes the name and that it makes him think of green meadows and snow-covered mountains and *The Sound of Music*. Her English is very formal, almost precise. He asks her how long she's been in New York.

"It will be two years next October. I have one more year of residency left. Then I will probably move to California, perhaps to Los Angeles. I am tired of cold winters."

He concurs with her weather analysis, but avoids noting his own disdain for Los Angeles. Some people love it there, yet her speech is so formal and L.A. so laid back that he finds it hard to picture her in such a place.

She begins to shiver and they agree to head back to the car. She's right, he thinks. If a fifty-degree day drives her indoors, it's time to live somewhere else.

"Would you take my picture before we go?" she asks as they stand, but it is more a statement of fact, a command as if she is the one who lives here, and he the visitor. She pulls a camera phone from her bag and shows him where to press for the digital photo. She stands several feet away, the water some hundred feet behind her, a turbulent boil with white froth in the far background. He snaps a photo and she checks it. He has caught a broad, white smile, enhanced by an overhead midday sun.

"Now you," she says. "If you give me your e-mail address, I'll send it to you."

He reluctantly moves from the bench and hands her the camera phone. He has never liked posing, but agrees. He stands with his feet spread and his arms akimbo. He tries to smile and feels relief when the shot is taken. She shows him the image, an olive-complexioned, dark-haired middle-aged man in a white button-down long-sleeved shirt and dark pants. The likeness is actually flattering. His age barely shows.

"Are you Jewish?" she asks after they have settled in the car's front seat.

He doesn't hear such a question often. Certainly not in New York. It is, however, not a new sensation. He is a Jew and Jews are integrated into the fabric of American life, yet there is an uneasiness that sits there. His family has been here for more than a hundred years, but nothing is settled. The Nazis had no qualms about killing Jews who had lived in Germany for centuries.

The woman's words are innocent enough. He answers, "Yes," and she goes on, oblivious to what flicks through his mind.

"My family is Muslim," she says, "But I practice nothing. If religion is about morality and ethics, you can certainly have that without any ritual. Do you agree?"

He nods. His slight unease withdraws into a corner and all but disappears. Yet he is reluctant to let the matter rest.

"Why did you ask if I was Jewish?"

"Oh, there are so many Jewish doctors at the hospital, and you are somehow like them—friendly, certainly intelligent, but also a bit reserved and cautious. They often talk about Jewish guilt. Is that something all Jewish men feel?" She smiles at her own words, almost daring him to explain.

Perhaps she is now the psychiatrist playing games, he thinks. He shrugs, yet feels the onset of guilt as she speaks. The woman is flirting with him, but he knows that no matter how appealing, he could never sleep with her, even kiss her, without torment. She is right—he has become cautious.

"How often do the buses go back to New York?" she asks. The segue releases him for a moment from thoughts about guilt. The question doesn't surprise him. They have only been together a bit more than thirty minutes. He is likely boring her. It's time for him to get home. A part of him feels relief. He checks his watch.

"There'll be one in about forty minutes. They have them all the time."

"I like that," she says. "Do you have the time to give me a short tour of the area?"

He feels trapped. "I guess I could do that," he answers with a tug of regret, as if he should have feigned some imaginary appointment, a technique years of business deception had ingrained.

"Oh, that would be very nice," she says in her clipped, very correct English.

"So I guess you speak Farsi and German as well as English?" he asks.

"What do you know about Farsi?" She raises one brown eyebrow.

"I've done business in Iran. I've been to Tehran, I think at least three times. And once to Khoramshahr to check on a cargo of steel pipes we sold. Business with NIOC, the National Iranian Oil Company."

"While the shah was still there?" she asks.

He nods.

"All the senior people there were tied to the shah's family. Everyone had a chance to make money."

"Except the traders who sold to them," he answers, but it is a throwaway line. Everyone made money then. Still, he has an urge to verbalize one of his memories of those days. "Every time we had a contract they would keep coming back and ask us to adjust our terms so there would be more graft to share. I remember one time when they said our sales price was actually too low. Can you imagine a state company telling a supplier to raise its price?"

She doesn't answer. He wants to ask her what her father did in Iran, but he says nothing. Obviously her family has some money. Vienna is an expensive city and she's gone to medical school. Perhaps her family was even one of the many he assisted in illegally transferring assets out of the country. There were strict rules against cash transfers, but Posner and his associates devised a scheme that enabled rich Iranians to buy commodities for export—copper, aluminum or steel scrap, it didn't matter. As soon as the export left an Iranian port, the title documents were negotiable and the traders in Rotterdam were more than happy to pay slightly below market price, which Posner passed on to the Iranian family's European bank account, less a reasonable commission. Maybe she's even somehow related to the shah's family. So many of the prosperous Iranians he worked with claimed such a connection.

"Look to your right," he says as they pass a large house that straddles more than a hundred feet of beachfront. He pulls to a stop and they absorb the tall twin cedar turrets that flank the extensive floor-to-ceiling glass windows.

"It's magnificent," she says. "Do you live near here?"

The question should not have been a surprise, but it is.

"Around the corner," he answers. His pulse quickens. She is pushing too far, but her flattery disarms him.

"Can I see it?" she asks.

She is over the line now. He has only to answer, "No," and everything will be formal and polite, but he quickly says, "Oh, sure."

He moves the car less than a hundred feet and turns the corner. He wonders, almost absurdly, whether she hears the sudden rush of blood that moves through his body, sees the nervous minispasms in his fingers as they clutch the wheel, or the fine line of moisture that settles above his upper lip, but all she says is, "Oh, what a pretty street."

He directs the car up his driveway and stops. He lets the engine idle, and they sit for a moment. The ocean beats a cadence against the sand and there is the odd, shrill cackle of birds, but the air is otherwise quiet. He sighs, ready to move the Lexus into reverse, but she interrupts his idea of escape and asks, "Can I see the inside?"

Even before he thinks of an answer, she is pulling the door handle open.

"Take care on the steps," he says. "They've just been refinished."

He slips his loafers off in the entrance and watches as she slides off her white sandals as well. He notices for the first time that her toes are coated with deep burgundy polish.

"I like to do what the host does."

Her words drip with unvarnished innuendo. At the top of the stairs she turns and surveys the area.

"The view is great."

Then she surprises him by ignoring the view as she walks around the room, touching small sculptures, and analyzing a succession of wood-block prints and lithographs on the wall farthest from the windows.

"Do you live here alone?" she asks

"Most of the time," he answers truthfully. "I'm married, but my wife spends most of her time in Manhattan."

She shrugs. He believes she doesn't care. The more she speaks, the more he comes to believe she is a latent free spirit, a throwback to the sixties, someone who would have rolled naked in the mud at Woodstock, screwed her brains out for a week, and only then went off to medical school. She continues to survey the room. There is a tightening in his chest as he thinks of her naked in Woodstock or here on the forest-green couch. An intense urge begins to grip his body. He has to think of something else. Now. He turns away and imagines the ocean two hundred feet beyond the window. He thinks of the last big storm that blew shingles off his roof. He considers these things until the urge passes. He realizes more fully that this is a mistake. She shouldn't be here.

"Where is this from? It looks like this house."

He needs to turn his head to see her standing in front of the pen-and-ink sketch of this very house. A rough design he made over twenty years ago and showed to an architect who liked the idea. He bought the land only after the architect agreed to design plans to fit the sketch. The drawing hangs on the wall leading to the master bedroom.

"It's my design," he says. "It's this house."

"*Ach, fantastish,*" she says. He is happy to show off something that is his alone. He ignores the fact that she speaks German.

She walks toward him and asks if she could have something to drink. "Perhaps some red wine," she suggests.

"I guess I can do that," he says, but there is edginess in his answer. He feels as if he is sliding into a deep pit without a handhold.

"Very nice, thank you," she answers, "but can I first use your bathroom?"

He points to the end of a short corridor. "The door on your left." She picks up her bag and moves in the direction he points. He hears the water running and the toilet flush. She is there for several minutes, but he gives it little thought. He spends the interval choosing a wine.

When she returns, he tells her about the sketch he made years ago as he pulls the cork from a bottle of Merlot. He pours a modest serving into a single glass. He has no intention of joining her. He holds the glass in his left hand and walks to where she has stopped, in front of the deep-green couch.

"Please sit," he says as she takes the glass. She takes a large sip, almost emptying the glass. He sits on the opposite couch and looks straight ahead through the large window at the ocean.

"Please sit over here," she says. "You seem so far away."

Posner moves to the other couch, just as she asks, "Can I rest my feet here?"

He waves his arm to the side in a universal gesture. She raises her hips and both legs spring forward onto the couch. She crosses one leg over the other and he faces ten polished toes. Then she shifts her legs back in parallel. She reallocates her skirt so that he has a clear view of her browned upper thigh. She spreads her legs more than slightly. The invitation is clear.

They talk aimlessly. She sits on the couch, ignoring the view, chatting about her hospital duties, her parents in Vienna, and why she doesn't want to stay in New York. He becomes edgy. He wants her to leave.

"Do you like my polish?" she asks, sliding her body down and raising one foot, barely inches from his face. The temptation is there, but he abruptly stands before she makes contact.

"I think we should go," he says.

She rises and follows him slowly to the top of the stairs. He feels her stare, but his eyes are fixated on her painted toes.

"Can I see you again?" she asks.

She smiles, doesn't wait for an answer, and searches her large straw bag, until she withdraws a card printed with her name and a New York number. Then she offers her hand, a puny gesture, he thinks, but he takes it anyway.

"I'd like to see you again," she repeats. "Whenever you want. Whatever you want to do."

Whatever is the only way something could happen, he thinks, but while there is more than a flicker of interest, he isn't crazy enough to start. He knows that a fuck in the room not twenty feet away from where they stand is where it would end. That's what whatever means. She was right about guilt, though. He feels it squeezing him like a fog that has crept into the room, filling every available space and daring, even mocking him to try to touch her. He wants to release her hand, but she holds his with even more pressure.

He sees from the quickening in the rise and fall of her chest that her breath comes in shorter increments. The pink dress fabric strains forward and he feels his cock swell. He looks away, out through the window, across the pine-coated dunes, as he's done only minutes before. Anything to forget the surge that has gripped him. He knows that she only has to brush against his groin and he would be lost, but then she eases the pressure on his hand and the rush begins to ebb.

"I have a boyfriend," she says. "His name is Henry, but I do like to meet other men."

Posner wants to hear none of this. Not the fact that there is a boyfriend who must surely suck on her painted toes. He had a second cousin named Henry, a gangling, acne-faced teenager when he last saw him more than forty years ago. The name merges with his memory's image of his cousin.

"Henry gave me this." She absently fingers a gold chain necklace from which hangs a small capital letter *H*. "To remember that both our names start with *H*."

"And what does Henry do?" he asks as if he might find some positive trait in the man sufficient to move her down the stairs and farther away from the bedroom.

"He's a resident in radiology. Also at Mt. Sinai."

Posner has regained his composure and has a sarcastic urge to say that Henry's balls were already probably burned away by radiation and that his sexual future was at best iffy, which is probably why she is here, but he says nothing. He feels her fingers slip away from his hand as she turns toward the steps.

"Is Henry Jewish?" he asks, and immediately realizes the banality of his words, yet she quietly says, "Yes, but he's not very religious." He hopes that perhaps she now realizes she shouldn't be here, and that her seduction was misplaced. It's time to go.

He pats the pocket with his keys, and then his eyes abruptly look down to his jacket. He moves his hands from one pocket to the other, stopping for a moment and then repeating the process.

"What's wrong?" she asks.

His hands stay in motion while his body turns to scan the floor, as if the object of his interest might somehow lie at his feet. He walks back to the couch and lifts the cushions before he comes back.

"Did you lose something?" At first he doesn't appear to hear, as he scans the floor, the kitchen counter, and the hallway.

"My wallet. Can't find my wallet. Dammit! I just went to the bank and took out a lot of cash. Goddammit! We've got to go. I must have dropped it at the beach or at Citarella's. Come on. First I'll drop you at the bus stop."

"I don't want to go just yet. Maybe after some more wine. Maybe when you get back."

Her smile teases him. She stretches here arms behind her head, which accentuates the swell of her breasts. Her mouth opens and her lips seem to ripen. She knows what she's doing, but he has no interest in such games. Not now. Not anymore.

"I said I want to go now." His voice rises.

He grabs at her upper arm, but she pulls away.

"Don't."

"Sorry. Look I don't have time for this. I'll be back soon, but be ready to leave when I get here."

He moves down the steps and out the door without looking back. He doesn't see her, but senses she still stands and watches him while he feels a mocking smile, until the closing door swallows the image.

It takes longer than the few minutes he'd hoped. The beach yields nothing, and so he drives to Citarella's. It's not under the table he sat at, and he goes inside and asks a cashier. She directs him to the manager who's on the phone. It's maddening. There's nearly five hundred dollars in the wallet, but he can't rush it.

"Yes, we found the wallet," the manager says without hesitation after the briefest of inquiries.

As his Lexus enters his own street, a car he doesn't recognize turns at the far corner. Another few weeks till summer and this street will be full of cars. His watch shows almost forty minutes have passed since he left. Dammit. What if Sara had called while he was out? He parks and leaves the car door open as he jogs up the front steps.

The door opens about three-quarters of the way and then stops. Something blocks further effort. Something heavy, but there's still enough room for him to easily enter.

She lays there without moving. Her eyes closed. He calls to her, but his voice is no more than an echo. At first he thinks she's playing some game with him, some final attempt at seduction, a stupid, vain idea, he later realizes, yet she looks so serene, lying there, composed in sensuality with one long leg stretched against a stair riser, as if she had been placed there by an artist, a bowl of fruit in a still life.

But then he sees blood seeping from the back of her head. He calls to her again without response. Then he shouts, as if a higher octave would make a difference. He draws a breath to calm himself and lifts one of her hands. The same one he held minutes before. The warmth is still there. He speaks to her now. Soft words that go unheard, but he continues. Then he reaches a finger toward her neck to check her pulse. He knows how to do this from a course in emergency medicine the firm gave some years ago.

He sits beside her, staring blankly at the entrance door, seeing nothing. He has no comprehension of what has just happened, so he cries. At one point he drops his head to her chest to check for a heart beat—uselessly. How could this have happened? How? How? But he knows. The stupid newly finished floors. Stupid. Stupid. He stands and wipes his face with his fingers. She is dead. Who should he call?

And then the reality begins to seep in.

# CHAPTER 2

He remains seated beside her and loses track of time. Through a blur he sees his watch. Three hours have elapsed since the bus arrived. His crying has stopped. He holds her hand. It's still warm, yet he senses stiffness in the fingers. A part of him realizes he should call someone, probably 911. He stands and moves his shaking body to the downstairs phone, but hesitates before he takes the instrument from its cradle.

What would they think? he wonders. It was an accident, but there is no proof. No witness to his sordid thoughts.

"It was just an accident," he shouts into the empty hallway. Yet some prosecutor might claim he bludgeoned her to death in a jealous, frustrated rage. What was she doing at his house? they would ask. Did she refuse you when you wanted sex? And Sara? She would ask the same thing and shout that she knew all along he was screwing someone else. And there would be no answer that could satisfy all of the questions. Even the complete truth would be insufficient.

"I wasn't even here," he shouts over and over again into empty space, and absurdly remembers the potential legal problems he faces. In those cases his innocence was suspect, but here, while there is no question, why would anyone believe him?

"This is madness," he says aloud, yet in some deep recess of his brain, in some effort at rationality, he has already decided he must find a way to move the body.

A storage shelf in the garage provides a supply of large steel-flexed trash bags. He takes two silver colored bags from the carton. He's about to leave when he impulsively grabs a pair of gardening gloves from the same shelf. He returns to the hall. She has not moved. He almost wished she had. He would pay the penalty if she survived, but she lies still and motionless. His tears return and he sits on the steps for several minutes until they dry.

He has never been this close to a dead person, but there is no particular discomfort. He slips on the gloves, and then lifts her body and tries to maneuver it into the bag. The body is all deadweight, a thought that in other circumstances might have brought a smile, but this is not such a time. The body moves surprisingly smoothly into the sack. Her face is the last part to be covered. Her eyes are closed as if in sleep.

"I'm so sorry," he says and lingers for a moment before he impulsively leans forward and brushes a kiss across her forehead. He starts to close the bag when he remembers her shoes. He takes the pair of white sandals, and slips them in as well. Then he slides the second bag around the first. It is actually a harder process that takes him several minutes. Perhaps the rigor has already begun. He rolls the bag over in the hallway and it seems secure.

Only then does he see her straw bag, as it hangs over the edge of a high step where its own fall must have ended, somehow immune from gravity's further demands. He brings the straw bag down and reopens the double plastic bags. He inserts the bag beside the lifeless form. His motion forces him to move his arm across the front of her body, necessarily across her breasts. He gulps down his bile and finishes his work, for that is what this has become.

That is when he sees the bloodstains for the first time. A purplish mass rests on the tiles where her head had landed. He finds a sponge, wets it, and begins to soak up the residue. Twice he flees back into the downstairs bathroom to vomit. He retches long after there is nothing left to expel, but the sight of her blood and other clotted matter that clings to the tiles is too much.

Many minutes pass before he concludes that the blood is gone, yet a small stain in the grout remains between some of the tiles. He curses silently and goes back to the garage for another remedy. He will bleach the grout he thinks, but there is no bleach in the laundry area. He could go out to buy bleach, or just clean the area as well as he could, and make up a story for Sara. Yes, that is what he'll do. The stain is too small for her to notice right away. The bleach will need to wait for another day. There will be many stories to concoct for Sara and others. He realizes with a stark revelation, as if a bright light has been turned on in a black room, that his deception has only begun, despite his absolute innocence.

Then he remembers the photo, his photo, still embedded in the memory of Heidi's cell phone. A cold sweat rises on his neck, and tightness invades his chest. He feels a rumbling in his body, something new and beyond anything he's ever felt. He knows he must again untie the plastic bags and retrieve the phone from her straw handbag.

First the outer one, and then the inside one. He sees her face again. What can change in a few minutes? he wonders. Yet she looks paler, as if the Iranian sun has begun to recede from her skin.

He pulls out the straw bag and removes the cell phone with the idea that later he will smash it into bits and distribute the scrap residue in the ocean. He reties the bag and stops.

He needs a plan. He needs to think. He walks upstairs and stares out the window at the ocean. The dark clouds have passed and the absence of motion at the tops of the sand pines tells him the wind has died. The sun hangs white, low, and alone to the west. Sara will be on her way to her Long Island meeting. He doesn't have much time, but his sense of logic and planning begin to return. He knows what he will do next, but first he washes the glass she used, returns it to the cabinet, and recorks the wine, which he leaves on the countertop. He stands at the top of the stairs, and then moves down toward the silvery bundle.

He's late getting to East Hampton Airport to pick up Sara. There's been just too much to do, too much to think about. He needed to put things as they should be before she comes. As he drives, he remembers how they met. It was her father who introduced them at a year-end cocktail reception at Posner's firm where her father's investment company was a client.

"Sara, this is Amos Posner, whose firm handles some of our overseas commodities business," Jacob Auslander spoke as one hand pressured Amos's elbow to turn.

Amos pivoted his body away from the open bar without the glass of red wine he'd ordered and faced a very tall brunette with shoulder-length hair, dark eyes, and a clear, pale complexion. She was wearing a simple black cocktail dress with a strand of tiny pearls and matching earrings. He absorbed all of this in seconds, even before Jacob introduced his daughter Sara.

"She's a lawyer. Just moved back east from Chicago."

Jacob went on for at least another minute, but Amos wasn't listening, only looking.

"Don't forget your wine," she said breaking into their mutual concentration.

Soon after they met, they discovered that she was coincidentally doing legal work for a British subsidiary of his firm. There was a chance meeting in London less than three months later. Three weeks after, they spent a weekend at Inverlochy Castle in Scotland and within six months they were married.

And now it's possible that the very survival of their marriage has come down to what's happened today and what he's done about all of it. He fights off a series of tremors that invade his hands, rubs sweaty palms on his pants, and wills himself to stay calm as he pulls up to the terminal entrance.

No one stands in front of the doors. He's late. The clock on the dash reads twenty past, yet she should be there. Should have already dropped the rental off. He leaves the car and steps a few feet inside the small terminal, which is nearly empty, but doesn't see her. Back in his car, he reaches for his cell phone to call, but a message is waiting. Sara called. Why didn't he hear the ring? Yet the reason is immediately obvious when he sees that the call came in earlier during that time when he was busy agonizing and then acting on a plan to remove the body. The message is harsh, almost cruel, as if she had spit the words out.

> *I'm not coming out tonight, or any time soon. And don't come back to town. I need some space. We need some separate time away from each other. Don't call. I'll be in touch when I think it's time to talk.*

That's it. Just a few lousy sentences. The words at first have the effect of instant paralysis. His throat tightens and his hands shake in uncontrolled frenzy. He sits without moving while the engine idles and he feels the heat in her voice. He plays the message over. Then again. One part of him might even have expected something like this after the way things were going, but not today. God, not today. He doesn't want to go back to the house, but he has to. He can't follow her back into the city much as he'd like to. He'll have to wait till she's ready. And maybe he's forgotten to clean up something back at the house. He drives back in a state of semishock, yet calms down enough to rationalize that it's better this way, isn't it? What would he say to her if she was here? If he told her the truth, she wouldn't believe him in a million years, not after all her recent suspicions. No, it's better this way. Just as long as it doesn't last, but he can't worry about that now.

✦ ✦ ✦

Three hours earlier, Amos had driven east to a scenic overlook parking area nearly three miles past the village of Montauk, a right-hand turnoff on the road to Montauk Point State Park. The overlook had views of the water and dunes, but at seven o'clock on an early May evening, dusk had begun to settle. A stand of pine trees at one end of the parking area had already morphed the asphalt into dark shadows when Posner pulled his car into the area.

The lot was empty. He drove to the darkened end where the car was largely hidden from the main road. He shut off the engine and rolled down the window. A few stray birds hooted into the dusk, but otherwise everything was quiet. This was the last moment he had to decide. He could still change his mind, but he had already thought everything through. There was no turning back.

He chose a level site more than a hundred feet away from the lot amidst a dense thicket of woods. The ground was covered with pine needles and other forest debris. This was why he brought the rake as well as the shovel. He worked quickly, as there was always the odd chance that his car might be spotted. He raked an area clean and then began to dig. The ground was soft from spring rains and he surprised himself when he managed to excavate to a depth of nearly three feet in only a half hour. His clothes were covered with soil and sweat stains by the time he walked back to the parking area. He almost expected to see a police cruiser waiting alongside his car, and slowly peered around a set of pine trees at the edge of the lot, but the area was quiet. Darkness had already fallen heavily across the overlook.

He opened the trunk and stared at the silver plastic package. That's all there is now, he told himself, just a package to be disposed of. The form was much heavier, much more rigid than when he first moved it to the car. He needed to partially squat to prop the body on his back. At first he staggered under the unbalanced load. He teetered backward three steps before he somehow switched his weight forward and stumbled ahead until he bumped into the open trunk. He steadied himself and cautiously shifted the weight across his right shoulder until he felt secure. He closed the trunk and began to walk into the woods, but his gait was uncertain. He wobbled as if drunk, barely able to control his motion until he realized that he could manage his movements far better by going from tree to tree.

He stopped after ten feet, leaned against a tree, and pulled the flashlight from his left-hand pocket to check on the location. The woods were dark now, although a faint twilight glow was still visible through the trees when he looked up. He was nearly back to the spot where he dug when he stumbled over a surface tree root. He fell forward and the body pitched to the ground as his arm lost its grip. The flashlight flew from his left hand. He heard a crack as it landed against a rock and everything turned black. He was engulfed in darkness.

He scrambled about in a panic. The bag was still there, just to his right, but he needed light to finish what he started. He had to finish. He couldn't just stop. He had to protect himself. There was no other way. He crawled to the left and stretched his hand in an arc that swept up branches, pebbles, twigs and pine needles. He kept on with his search. The flashlight couldn't have fallen too far. A tightness rose in his throat. He was about to stop and cry when his fingers touched a cylinder. He pulled it forward and sat up. He did the first thing he thought of. He shook the flashlight. Nothing except a rattle. Loose, he thought. Something was loose. He slid his right hand to the lens cover and slowly tried to turn the end that emitted the light. It moved. Nearly two turns later the light jumped out at him. He saw everything, the silver bag that rested on the ground, and only a few yards away, a mound of dirt that surrounded a trench.

He stood, but was so dizzy with relief he stumbled over the dark bag. When he rose again he began to drag the bag forward with one hand. There was no other way. He didn't have the energy to lift her anymore. He was nearly at the hole when the bag snagged on a root.

He heard a rip and focused the light downward. He saw a patch of pink that surrounded the partially torn-off white heel of a shoe.

He propped the light on the top of a log and slid the bag into the hole as gently as possible. There was no time for ceremony, but he would say something for her every day as long as he lived. He filled the hole and raked the ground over with pine needles and twigs, gathered his tools and made his way back to the parking area. As he closed the trunk over the shovel and rake, he saw a crescent moon rise above the trees to the east.

As soon as he entered the car, the rearview mirror glared back at him with a red slash across his cheek. His face and arms were covered with soil. Bits of twigs and damp leaves clung to his shirt and pants. He checked his watch. There was barely enough time to get home to shower and change before he needed to meet Sara. He was already moving westward, toward his home, every mile confirming his innocence, when he stretched his right arm forward and opened the glove compartment to replace the flashlight. That's when he saw the phone. Heidi's cell phone was still there, a small gray oval he had yet to eliminate. He rechecked his watch. There wasn't time to dispose of it the way he wanted. He laid it on the seat next to him. There would be time to do it properly tomorrow morning. There was no need to rush.

He opened the window and swallowed cool air. He started to relax as he neared the street where he needed to turn to reach his house. That's when the cell phone began to ring.

# CHAPTER 3

He stays in Amagansett and waits for the police to investigate. He has only had a few brief conversations with Sara and has not yet been back to the city, but she's indicated that his banishment may only be temporary. All he can do is wait, yet the Heidi episode weighs him down so heavily that he barely thinks of anything else.

The police visit isn't a surprise. Posner has thought about the possibility since it all happened. At one point, however, some four weeks after the accident, for that is what he had come to call Heidi's death in his own mind, without waver or compromise, he almost believes that there will be no investigation. He has mentally willed himself into anonymity with the same absurdity that one buys a lottery ticket and believes, during the trip home that they will be the big winner.

His other self, the more rational corporate analyst, has decided within days after the accident that he will likely be contacted. There were probably no more than twenty people on the bus on that morning. The bus line keeps a computer record of all passengers for each trip. Someone will report her absence. Perhaps hospital staff would have already raised an alarm when she failed to arrive for her shift the next day. Perhaps she even had a date with Henry that night and he might have personally checked her apartment. A missing person's whereabouts would be followed up. The authorities would discover her planned trip to East Hampton. They would endeavor to speak to anyone who might have had contact with her. Then there also was the conversation on the bus just before she exited. That might have also been observed, and it likely was.

And so, one part of his brain, had begun his defense, that of anonymity, and he imagined, even prerehearsed what he might tell the police.

"Yes, I vaguely remember her. I think she wanted to know if the beach was near the bus stop. I told her it was too far to walk, and she should take a taxi, although that day, if I recall, was a bit chilly for the beach."

"No, I can't really remember what we spoke about. I think she said she was from somewhere in Europe and worked at some hospital."

"I'm sorry I can't recall any more. Didn't you say it was about a month ago? Hell, sometimes I can't recall who we elected to Congress."

"I've lived here over twenty years, but my wife works most days in Manhattan, and I'm back and forth."

And so it might go on. The only issue Posner hasn't considered is whether Heidi and he were seen at the outdoor table after he picked up lunch, but that whole encounter hadn't taken more than a minute. Moreover, he was grateful that the parking spaces in front of the store were actually taken, so that the sight of her entering his car in the rear lot would stand less likelihood of observation.

In fact, there is no telephone call from the police. A business card that introduces a Detective Wisdom is left in the crack of his door on a Tuesday morning while he swims in the indoor pool at Gurney's Inn Resort. Neat block lettering asks him to call at his convenience. Nothing else.

Two days later, the appointment arranged, Detective Peter Wisdom appears at Posner's door, and is invited upstairs. He seems to be in his late thirties, tall and slim with short light brown hair. He's dressed in a blazer, light-blue button-down shirt, a dark tie, and khaki chinos. Detective Wisdom acts like a neighbor and freely announces he has fifteen years service in the East Hampton Police Department. He even offers that he is married with a young son and lives in Sag Harbor, one of the small hamlets that are part of the town of East Hampton. As a local resident as well as a police officer, he seems to know the subtle nuances of life in the town. Posner feels an initial unease, yet Wisdom appears completely calm as the conversation moves forward. He steers the discussion as if they were new acquaintances at the local VFW hall.

"We've had this fax from the NYPD," he says, after several minutes of small talk. He pulls a few pages from his jacket pocket. "A missing person report. A woman went to East Hampton almost four weeks ago and then vanished. Her boyfriend filed the report. We know she was on the same bus as you on that day. That's from the bus records. They keep a computer record of all passengers, so we're checking on anyone who might have seen her. Strictly routine."

Wisdom holds out the papers. Posner reaches for them tentatively, as if they might scorch his fingers, but he takes them and pretends to read the diminished print. There is nothing in the text he does not already know, but he consciously takes his time. The second page has a grainy photo. Heidi is standing on a balcony with a man, although most of his body and face have been cropped. Probably Henry, Posner thinks. Her face on the copy appears faded, as if she has already died; yet Posner manages to examine the documents without an obvious tremor invading his fingers.

"So this woman is a doctor," he says after a few minutes, somewhat proud of himself for his control. "We could always use more doctors out here."

Wisdom smiles and nods agreeably. "But only if we can find them."

This last comment alerts Posner. Some small bell rings in his head. Detective Wisdom has done his homework. Posner feels wariness, as if there is the possibility of some trap out there. Wisdom knows Posner was on the same bus, and also that Heidi had spoken to him, probably from the driver. The questions that follow, however, were less intrusive than what Posner had imagined.

He says he vaguely remembers the woman because she asked him how to get to the beach from the bus stop and is unaware of any other conversations she had. He feels he has covered himself with a veneer of truth. In five minutes it is all over. Wisdom writes down Posner's New York City phone number as well the one in Sara's office.

"It's useful to know how we can reach potential witnesses," Wisdom says, strictly methodical, like an accountant doing an audit. The comment makes Posner wonder whether Wisdom knows he has pending issues with the Justice Department, but the idea seems far-fetched.

"Well, thanks for your help," Wisdom says as they walk down the stairs.

Posner opens the front door, yet finds it impossible to ignore the presence of Wisdom standing on the very tiles where Heidi's head split open. He wills himself into calm, yet feels the tremor of nausea rising in his throat.

"Sorry I couldn't be of more help," he says as he pushes the door farther open.

"It's part of the process," answers Wisdom. "We'll call you again if we have any more questions. Thanks for your time. We know you've lived here for a number of years, so we won't bother you again if we don't have to."

Posner shakes the offered hand and immediately worries that his fingers were too damp or even trembling, but if so, Wisdom seems to take little notice. As soon as the door closes, Posner races to the nearest bathroom, gagging uncontrollably, but it was not until three hours later that he'd wondered whether Wisdom might have heard his spasmodic retching from the driveway.

✦ ✦ ✦

Posner realizes that innocence may be a state of mind long before it becomes a legal issue. An observer may only glimpse a part of the truth, yet all sorts of preconceived views stir the pot of judgment. A day after Wisdom left, Posner remembers a vacation he and Sara had taken some ten years before to Israel. They stayed at a hotel on the Sea of Galilee. On the Friday morning they arrived, the hotel was already busy with Israelis away for the weekend, but by late Saturday afternoon most of the locals were gone, as Sunday was a workday.

He and Sara lounged on adjoining chaises. At five in the afternoon, the lake shimmered in dwindling sunlight. The large pool, so filled just a day before with vacationers, was empty. A small tote bag stuffed with their wallets, credit cards, passports, and plane tickets rested under his chaise.

They had treated themselves to a bottle of a decent local white wine, and by the second glass they had both eased into languid drowsiness, that never-never land barely a breath or two above sleep, impervious to all the traditional worries that flood daily life.

And they both knew, without a word, that later, after raising themselves from drowsiness, there would be sex in the large bedroom with a view of the lake. And after showers there would be a quiet dinner of salad and St. Peter's fish on the restaurant terrace, alone except for a few other random visitors and the odd waiter.

He was on the edge of a dream when the shouts roused him. The words were in English, so there is no mistake in their purpose. A security guard on the far end of the pool shouted, "Stop him. Stop the thief."

Posner sat up, followed the guard's pointed arm and looked to the far end of the grounds. A boy was running away, no more than a flash of thin dark arms in the twilight, but there was enough light to see that the boy clutched Posner's recognizable beige bag in one hand as he sprinted across a long stretch of small jagged boulders that bordered the hotel grounds. At first Posner stared in some awe as the boy glided effortlessly across the stones, an animal species that levitated above the sharpest edges, and then he raised himself upright and began to scream.

"Catch him! Catch him!"

Only then did he spring from the chaise and begin to run after the boy. Another guard at the edge of vision moved into a slow trot, at best barely a performance gesture, and without energy.

Posner ran after the boy and quickly became the lead pursuer. The boy had somehow approached the chaise and snatched his bag. Posner could not allow such a theft without some action. The boy turned once to check his pursuers. There was a brief flash of dark arms and hair before he ducked behind a rock outcropping.

Posner continued to run, but he was barefoot and the sharp rocks cut flesh from his instep. He had been violated, and the pain from the rocks soon slowed his pace and a security guard easily passed him. He finally pulled to a stop and bent over. He felt his legs wobble as if in spasm. Just as he straightened up, he saw his bag between two large rocks no more than ten feet away. The thief had dropped it while making his escape. He checked the contents. Everything was there. He turned back toward the hotel and saw Sara standing near where the rocky boundary began. He waved to her as he held the tote above his head and jammed his thumb in the air.

A noise from behind caused him to turn back. The security guard was standing next to a boy. The guard began to slap him again and again. The boy soon fell to the ground and the guard then kicked him repeatedly. There was a scream and then silence. It was all over in seconds. The guard turned and looked back to where Posner stood. Posner held the bag in the air and the guard offered a weak smile and began to walk toward him.

"Why were you hitting him, and why didn't you call the police?" asked Posner.

"They're all the same. Fucking Arab thieves. We couldn't prove anything so this is the best way to treat them," was all the guard said.

As they walked back together, Posner looked over his shoulder and saw the boy stand and walk toward a group of similar age. He watched the guard peel away back to his post on the far side of the pool while he massaged his right hand with his left.

The next morning as they checked out, the hotel manager told Posner that the actual thief was an Israeli boy from the neighborhood who had a recent history of such actions. The boy's father found out and advised them early that morning, but the hotel declined to call in the police.

"His father will discipline him, and that is enough," the manager said. At Sara's suggestion, Posner had started to ask about the other boy, the innocent Arab boy, but thought better of raising the issue. "What good would it do?" he later asked her. "It's a cultural thing, and innocence is not always what it seems to be."

Ten days after Detective Wisdom's visit, Posner sits alone in the living room of the Manhattan apartment watching television. Sara has consented to let him back in the apartment for a few days at a time, and he's grateful she doesn't raise the old issue of his fidelity. She asks him to sleep on the living room sofa bed. He doesn't argue and just accepts that he must somehow gradually regain her trust.

"Television is a good way to quickly decompress," she's always said when they'd drink wine and watch together, but she isn't here now, and he thinks that the glass of Merlot he sips is probably a more effective path to decompression. The show is one of the newer crime-scene spin-offs that have lately invaded the networks. A police forensic team is searching a car for evidence of an old homicide. One of the cops uses a glow-in-the-dark chemical to reveal blood traces, although the suspected crime occurred years before.

The cop's partner remarks, "We wouldn't even have a shot at

getting these results without probable cause giving us a chance to search the car."

The words stay with Posner long after he goes to bed. Probable cause. What does it really mean? he wonders as he tosses for several hours before exhaustion plunges him into oblivion.

As soon as Sara leaves the next morning, he checks the Internet for information. The chemical referred to in the program that glows when applied to blood is called Luminol. It's been used for some time by crime-scene investigators to detect traces of blood. The only apparent way to avoid a positive test result is to rip out the contaminated surface in its entirety. There is scant chance of even such simple renovation of a few tiles without involving Sara, since the entrance area was redone only three years before. He used bleach to remove all surface stains from the tiles and grouting, but the blood traces are still there, an image his mind cannot release, and he begins to wonder whether he will ever be liberated.

His Internet search yields one small, but unconvincing, consolation. He uncovers a comment from a defense attorney, which suggests that Luminol can produce a fake blood positive when it reacts with other substances including vegetation and cleaning fluid.

He waits till nearly ten to call Mark Rothman, his attorney. They haven't spoken for several months, which is a positive sign with regard to his corporate uncertainties. Still, he needs to speak to Mark. His attorney specializes in criminal law, albeit only white collar, as far as Posner knows. He realizes they could speak in privileged circumstances, but he is not anywhere prepared to share his secret. He is kept on hold for several minutes until a secretary announces that she'll put him through.

"This is Mark," grumbles a voice. Posner pictures the slightly built man with a pink scalp sitting in his black leather chair, feet raised on the far corner of the desk, an unlit pipe stem clutched in the corner of his mouth.

"You didn't need to call. Nothing's happening, and that's good news." Mark's voice is clearer now. Posner imagines that the pipe has moved to Mark's hand, or even to the desktop.

"I just wanted to check in," says Posner. "It's been a while."

"Like I said, there's no problem. Anything else I can do for you today?"

Posner feels he is being rushed off the phone, yet he realizes the man is not a friend, so he keeps his response brief.

"Oh, I was just curious about something," answers Posner. "When the authorities want to investigate something or someone, and they need a search warrant, what does probable cause mean?"

"There's nothing I can imagine you have to worry about on that score," answers Mark. "As far as probable cause, shall I check the law dictionary, or can you get the short version?"

"The short version will work."

"Okay, then. The gist of it is that if the authorities feel there are reasonable grounds for an evidence search based on the circumstances, a judge will grant the warrant."

Posner is silent for several seconds before speaking. "I thought the phrase was probable cause, but you said reasonable grounds. What's the difference?"

"None really, except that some decision about ten years ago seems to have expanded the authorities' ability to search. In fact it's not too hard now for the Feds or even local cops to get a warrant. I mean if someone's innocent, then they have nothing to hide. Right?"

A part of Posner would like to spend more time in New York City. It is a conscious mental effort to distance himself from the accident. The city is not unfamiliar. He had worked there for years. But with

Sara's current mood, he's forced to opt for the solitude of his house on the end of Long Island in spite of the disturbing memories that greet him whenever he opens the front door.

He prefers to think about the positive side of staying at the beach. The house is in an area that has other advantages: the broad sandy beaches, the ocean that shifts and amazes him with every tidal surge, and the sea terns that glide and swoop for prey among the small fish or mollusks along the surf. But most of all he savors those days when the weather rises up and feeds the air with the raw energy of a storm. Not a hurricane, for sure, but the wild uncontrolled release of passion that only some act of nature can bring; a happening that boils the ocean into a frenzy and diminishes the role of man who must hunker down amidst the torrent and wait to see if there will be another day. He loves all of this, but now is torn between avoiding the house and staying in New York, but this decision is now controlled by Sara. His mind foolishly tells him that by living a hundred miles away in the city, the wall of concrete and brick buildings will somehow insulate him from what rests under the ground at the Montauk Overlook.

Perhaps the city would be easier to take if things between him and Sara were more normal, but this isn't the reality of their relationship. It also seems that she can only tolerate his New York presence in small doses, as if her forgiveness of his presumed betrayal can only be earned in similar micro measures. He accepts this as the only way to heal their relationship. The consequence of this arrangement is that he's really left with no choice at all about where to spend most of his time.

He constantly thinks about the late spring rains. He checks the weather daily in the papers and on the Weather Channel. When heavy rain is forecast across the eastern end of Long Island, and especially over the isolated area where Heidi's body rests, his chest falls away as the prospect grows that the water will slowly erode his secret.

He imagines the topsoil washing away, until someone, a hiker, or his dog, even a fox or deer pulls away at one end of an exposed end of plastic bag until some appendage is exposed. He has a compelling urge to drive back to the overlook and walk through the brush to see if his secret is still safe, but he has so far resisted such impulse.

"There was a message for you on the tape," Sara says. This is his second day back on this visit and it is a rare recent incident of direct interaction. She speaks as she sits at a small desk in the living room opening her order from the Vietnamese take-out. Amos sits across the room on a couch that faces the muted sounds from a flickering television. This arrangement is typical of their recent physical separation whenever they are both in the apartment.

Posner has spent the day at the Neue Galerie on Fifth Avenue staring at the erotic drawings of an Austrian artist named Egon Schiele who only lived until he was twenty-eight. There was boldness in the artist's renderings. Women subjects unflinchingly part their legs to reveal crimson labia, and all of it makes Posner uncomfortable as he imagines some connection between these provocative poses and Heidi.

"A Detective Wisdom from the East Hampton Police asked you to call him back. What's that all about?"

Her sudden interest is a change from the recent past and catches him off guard. He raises a glass of wine to buy time. He sips the burgundy liquid and leans back. He must tell the smallest part of the story now, and he isn't sure how to do it. The words finally come out as if he were another person speaking.

"Oh, there was this person on the Hampton Jitney that went missing some time ago. A woman. She was on the same bus I took, so the town police wanted to know if I could help them."

"Did you already speak to them?'

"Yeah. About a week or two ago. The detective I spoke to said he'd probably have a few more questions. No sweat."

Sara doesn't comment. She just turns away from him with apparent disinterest and digs her chopsticks into a container of spicy chicken with cashew nuts.

Wisdom answers on the first ring.

"This is Amos Posner. You left a message for me to call."

"Thanks for getting back so fast. Not everyone's so good about responding."

Posner pictures Wisdom sitting at a battered metal desk in a dingy room filled with smoke, and then catches himself in mid-thought. There is a brand new police department building in East Hampton. The desks are likely all new and smoking has surely been banned.

This is not some old film or television image.

"How can I help you?"

"I have a few more questions you might help us out with. Can I ask when you plan to be back in Amagansett?"

"I'm really not sure," answers Posner. "Give me a second."

He realizes that a hundred miles cannot separate him from this matter. Nor a thousand. Seconds of dead air follow. He sighs, but is sure Wisdom doesn't hear him.

"The day after next," he says.

"Can I come over about ten in the morning?" asks Wisdom. It is a formality, which Posner readily agrees to. There is no other option. He must play out his story to the end. He tells Sara he is going back to Amagansett the next day.

"Whatever," is all she says, but her shrug reveals indifference. Still, he feels that even her verbalized apathy seems to be an improvement.

"Did you notice if the woman had a cell phone?" asks Wisdom.

The detective is dressed in similar clothes to those he wore on his first visit. Posner absently wonders if the man has multiple similar outfits, or whether he never changes his clothes. He opts for the former, but the idea brings a smile to his lips, which he cannot disguise.

"Something funny about the question?" asks Wisdom.

"Sorry," answers Posner. "Something unrelated. I apologize."

Wisdom grunts and pulls a pad from his coat pocket.

"What about it? Did you see her with a cell phone?"

"I'm pretty sure I didn't," says Posner. "We only spoke for a few seconds. You're not supposed to use a cell phone on the Jitney."

Wisdom nods. Something in his manner makes Posner definitely realizes the man is a long way from some bumbling cop. He is more like that shrewd, yet modest, television detective he watched years ago. That's it, Colombo. Except that Wisdom has neither a cigar nor a raincoat.

"It seems she made a call to her boyfriend. Another doctor. A guy named Henry Stern sometime that afternoon. The day she disappeared. Said she was calling from some nice house in the area with ocean views."

Wisdom puts his notepad down and his eyes rise to see through the floor-to-ceiling windows.

"Lots of houses out here have ocean views," is all Posner thinks of saying, but it is the right comment.

"You're right about that," says Wisdom and returns his gaze to his notebook.

As Wisdom studies his notes, Posner's memory fixates on the cell phone. The incessant ringing on the front seat of his car, until the last chimes die away, and his ultimate race the next morning to a local beach where he finds a stone and pummels the amalgam of plastic and metal into tiny bits; and then the drive to the town recycling center later that day to scatter the remnants, then little more than powder, amidst the piles of nonrecycling garbage; the chicken bones, orange peels, and assorted household waste that have become man's footprint.

But the cell phone only rang sometime after seven that evening, he remembers. She must have called Henry earlier. From his house. It had to be from his house. When she was in the bathroom, but she used her cell phone, not his house phone. That's good. Very good. So there is no further basis to connect him with Heidi except that his house has an ocean view, but as he explains to Wisdom, such a vista is far from unusual in the area.

Wisdom rises to leave. Thanks him again for his time and help. There is no hint of nausea this time when Wisdom moves across the tile floor toward the door. Posner begins to believe he is getting past all of this, and that he is not only in the clear, yet beyond any evidence to remotely connect him to Heidi. He breathes deeply and goes upstairs. He pours a glass of wine. That night he sleeps deeply and late into the next morning. He has two weeks of such mindless solitude.

And then he gets a visit from Dr. Henry Stern.

# CHAPTER 4

Dr. Henry Stern is a tall man, over six feet, with straight brown hair and green eyes. He is thirty-two when he first meets Heidi at a hospital Christmas party a year before.

"Do you celebrate Christmas?" she asks her voice throaty and European accented, as she sips a glass of eggnog.

They stand with two other staff members in white coats and a well-dressed man who announces he is in administration. Stern shakes his head slightly.

"No. I'm Jewish. By the way that's not spiked, you know," he says pointing to her glass as she looks up at him, her dark eyes wide as globes.

"Spiked?"

"I mean there's no booze in it. No liquor at all. Can't have the hospital pushing alcohol during business hours."

The others all laugh, and he did mean it as a joke, since business hours equaled a twenty-four-hour day, but her eyes seize his and stop his own laughter. That's when he turns away, as he feels a flush creep across his face. He drifts across the room and joins two other radiologists, but for a change he doesn't feel like discussing shadows on x-rays; the indications of something ranging from either benign to inoperable. He has learned to control his emotions when he speaks with patients and their primary physicians. He has built up a wall of false bravado during such conversations, always faking the positive, which will give them a tortured future of discomfort and occasional pain as well as hope.

He doesn't know her name, but steals looks across the room for the next half hour until he sees her standing alone near the door. He summons some hidden reserve of courage and approaches.

"Leaving so soon?" he asks and feels the flush return to his face. When she looks at him again with those black eyes, he begins to sense he is lost. Utterly lost or bewitched, it doesn't matter.

They go to a neighborhood bar a few blocks away. Tiny Santa dolls share space on the shelves alongside gin and Scotch bottles. All-too-familiar Christmas songs are piped through a pair of speakers at the front of the room. A tiny tree at the end of the bar winks red-and-green lights. They laugh at the juxtaposition of Santa and the alcohol, and she wonders how he can safely drive a sled with a drinker's red nose. They laugh some more and keep walking until they reach an empty booth in the back. He asks for a beer, and she takes a glass of red wine. They both order burgers.

"I thought Muslims don't eat meat?" he asks referring to her cultural disclosure during their walk.

She cuts the air with a wave of her hand.

"That's a Hindu thing, but I do many things Muslim women don't do." She stares intently at him, and then goes on.

"Beef should be all right for Muslims if the slaughter is ritual and clean. We are also not supposed to eat pork. The same as Jews, part of halal or Muslim dietary rules. It's the high level of uric acid in the pig that is of concern. But I confess I do like wine. Alcohol is discouraged, but one can't be perfect."

She sips her wine before she adds, "Adultery is also forbidden, except that I'm not married."

Then she laughs and her cackle overrides the dim Christmas music that floats from the front of the room. She describes how she is a blend of three cultures; her parents' Iranian background, her years growing up in a rather strict Austrian world, and the much more laissez-faire American world, especially in New York.

"And which do you prefer?" he asks.

His earlier disorientation, for that's what it was, has gone. He is now the consummate successful New York male his ego has constructed. And she knows nothing about him, with or without his private medicinal blanket, a condition he isn't about to tell her. He wants to gain this woman's serious interest. He hesitates to speak to avoid making dumb comments, yet when she reaches out and touches his hand, his voice all but disappears.

"I think I prefer it here," she says, her accent deeper than before.

He stares at the generous hint of brown cleavage that rises above her scooped sweater neck, and calls for another round to mask the sound of blood rushing through his body. He wonders if she can hear the pumping. All his training tells him she can't, yet she must see his fingers shake slightly as they grasp the new beer glass. She must see the white foam spill over the rim as he raises his glass.

"Prosit," she says. "That's how we toast each other in Vienna."

Later he trembles when she takes his hand and leads him into her studio apartment only a block from the hospital. A bed, a small sofa, a table wedged against the wall. She says it's enough space.

"What do you like to do?" she asks, as the sweater rises above her head and flies away.

When he doesn't answer, and just stares at her, she says, "Then let me show you what I like."

Later they speak long into the night about the Middle East. She abhors the mullahs that govern modern Iran, and he detects that part of her enmity was based on how her family had been treated. She dislikes the Israelis, not, she protests, because they were Jews, but because of the way they abuse the Palestinians. She had read Tolstoy and Shakespeare, and they laughed together when he remembered the bard's quote about first killing all the lawyers, as a reason for their both becoming doctors.

"After all," she said more than once when she rolled on top of him, "Doctors have to stick together."

Henry waits for her at a table against the far back wall of Luca's on First Avenue. That's where they always meet for dinner. He watches as diners come in, most of them locals like him, there for the fish stew, or the tagliatelle with duck ragout, which is his own favorite.

Heidi has agreed to meet him at eight, but it is already past nine. He's already finished two glasses of the house Chianti. He wonders if she's standing him up on purpose. When they last met, two nights before, the evening had become a disaster. When she was ready for sex he just couldn't perform. At first she was angry and threw curses at him in German. Then she softened somewhat.

"It happens sometimes," she said, but still steered him to the door.

Yet he knew why the problem arose. A week before he had seen her emerge from a private office looking disheveled, her lipstick slightly smeared and her hair in disarray. A tall young intern followed her. He could have killed her at that moment, but all he wanted to do was lose himself within her body. He realized that he needed to calm down, but when the next opportunity came, he couldn't do it.

There is a state of hopelessness when obsessive love becomes uncontrollable. People in love generally share some aspects of life; culture, music, books, art, even political discussion, or debate, but she would have none of that. She wanted to fuck away their time together, and he became a slave to that excess. Yes. That's what he had become, a toy, a plaything. She was a psychiatrist, and had pushed his buttons for her own gratification, as well as her sense of control. There was even more to it. One night, about a month before, Heidi had more than her usual quota of wine.

On reflection, he wasn't all that surprised when she said, "I like Jewish men. They're both very intelligent and oral. All my life I've heard how Jews outperformed the general population in academics, business, law, and, particularly, medicine. Especially here in New York. It's a challenge for me to outperform them."

So Heidi is a user and a manipulator whose social goal seems to be to sexually dominate men, particularly Jewish men. But it didn't matter. All he cared about was the few times each week he could bury his face in her flesh. He knew she saw other men; she collected them like stamps, or coins, one-time stands of sex, but always Jewish men from what he came to observe, yet she stayed with him for the most part, and in some recess of his brain he somehow hoped she would stay there forever.

They were both off on the day when she said she wanted to take the bus to East Hampton, and she'd pointedly avoided inviting him to spend time with her until the evening. He was pissed and took it out on the Avis rental agent when he picked up the Chevy at mid-morning. A sudden impulse made him anxious to drive back upstate to where he grew up even though there were no relatives or friends still there. He just needed a break.

He took the Taconic Parkway and kept the radio on the classical music station until the hills delivered more static than music. He exited at the Hillsdale turnoff and drove around aimlessly, even past his old house, now expanded and likely modernized by the weekenders who had bought it from his father's estate, but it was shrouded behind a cluster of blue spruce much like his own past was hidden. He ate a sandwich at the Taconic Diner and headed back. He dropped the car off about five, and then went back to shower and change for dinner.

Ten o'clock passes, yet she hasn't come. The previous day she had told him she was taking the Hampton Jitney to East Hampton on her day off.

"Ever since I've been in New York people always talk about the Hamptons and the beautiful beaches out there."

So she went on an early bus despite the chill. After he got back to his apartment he checked his cell phone for messages. He had been so upset that morning he'd forgotten to take it with him. He saw that she had called. Since that day he played it over a hundred times.

*Just wanted you to know I'm out here at the beach. Actually, I'm in a house with a view of the ocean. I met this nice guy and he invited me in for a view. I might be a little late for dinner, but I should be there.*

And there wasn't anything more. He tried to call her that same day, in the early evening, probably shortly after dusk, but her phone rang until her message pickup. He tried again later but could never get through, even to her voice mail. Maybe she was out of the regular service area in one of those dead spots. She never came to the restaurant, but also didn't show up for her shift the next day. That was more surprising, as she was always diligent about her shifts.

The next afternoon he got a call from her supervisor. There was no secret about their relationship. "Do you know where she is?"

He somehow suspects that Heidi has found another partner. Another lover. The thought tears him up, as it has before. Another mouth seeking out and gliding above the brown skin, moving a tongue into her crevices, bringing her off. Still, it is not like her. Two more days pass. He convinces her superintendent to open her apartment, but there is no evidence she has been back. A toothbrush rests on the ledge of the sink, clumps of aqua caught in bristles, just next to the strands of dark hair that float above her hairbrush. He picks up the toothbrush and sucks the stiff blades into his mouth, but it isn't her. She's not there, and for the first time since they met, he feels a chill, and realizes with horrific suddenness that he may never see her again. That's when he decides to call the police.

✦ ✦ ✦

People appear to go missing in New York with amazing frequency, yet most are found. They turn up after a few days, or weeks, either after a drug or alcohol binge, or a tryst with a secret lover. They make excuses and apologize to the authorities.

The voice on the other end of Henry's call is reassuring.

"If she went to East Hampton for the day by bus, there will likely be a record. We'll check it out and ask the town police to look for her. Do you happen to have a recent photo?"

He does. They'd spent a long weekend in Bermuda three months before. He'd placed the camera on a balcony table, set the timer, and then taken a number of shots. He chooses one with her silhouetted against the balcony wall. She wears a new sleeveless pink-and-white dress that shows off her tan. Her short black hair barely grazes her cheek. He uses a scissors to slice away most of his own image and delivers the photo to the appointed address that afternoon.

He tells the investigator that he thinks her parents might live in or near Vienna, but that they should seek an Austrian address through the hospital since he doesn't have one and Heidi never spoke of them.

"No." As far as he knows she doesn't have any relatives that live in America.

And later, "I don't know if she had relationships with other men."

The last question raises an edge of angst. It wasn't possible that they might think he had anything to do with her disappearance, yet a tiny seed of doubt rises, and makes him tremble. He doesn't tell them about the message on his cell phone. Not then. He couldn't admit there could be other men.

They thank him and ask that he tell them if she turns up. From past experience they expect that would happen within a few weeks at most. In the meanwhile, they will check with the Hampton Jitney and advise East Hampton P.D. to be on the lookout. They've done this sort of thing before. Everything they do seems so routine to Henry, yet he lives on the edge for the next several weeks.

But time does not solve the problem. Eventually he goes back to the police and plays the cell phone message she left. They seem to pass off his original failure to provide the information as jealousy, which it was. He is advised that a detective named Peter Wisdom of the East Hampton Police still has the case file unless for some reason he'd turned it over to the Suffolk County Police Department, which handles major crimes. In this case, at least so far, there is no evidence yet of anything sinister. They tell him that Detective Wisdom has interviewed all the passengers who live in East Hampton who took the same bus as Heidi that morning. They give him Wisdom's direct number at work.

He thinks about this for a few more days and then decides to call the Hampton Jitney bus company directly rather than Wisdom. He wants to speak to the same passengers as well as the bus driver, but they deny him access to the lists. They say it's confidential information. He calls a lawyer he knows from their undergraduate days at Yale. Judah Cohen greets his call with collegial enthusiasm and arranges for an associate to provide him with an insight into the maze of a legal system that has simultaneously become America's strength and soft spot.

Several days later he speaks to Detective Wisdom to confirm that he can access the passenger list if he files a Freedom of Information Act request, called a FOIA. Anyone can do it. A citizen can look into reading Nixon's Watergate notes, the background behind Lyndon Johnson's Tonkin Gulf Resolution, aged FBI files on a relative or friend sucked into the McCarthy Senate hearings, or possibly even certain CIA communications to President Bush about potential problem weapons in Iraq.

Wisdom is forthcoming. "We prefer that private citizens not get involved, but to be honest, sometimes you people pick up things we miss. If you find out anything unusual, please let me know. Henry readily agrees to this and also offers to send Wisdom one of the photos of Heidi in the pink-and-white dress.

The process is not swift, yet moves along. In ten days he has the list of passengers, more due to Detective Wisdom's intervention than anything else. He recognizes none of the names. People who live in the New York area. Some of them in the town of East Hampton. He makes a copy of the list. He decides to start with the driver, who lives in a small town on the eastern end of Long Island, but the results are spotty.

"I wouldn't even have remembered her if the police hadn't asked some questions," the driver says. "There's not much I can add to what I told them. I think she spoke to a few people on the bus, but that was when she was getting ready to leave."

He doesn't really expect anything more. The bus driver clearly spent his time looking at the road ahead and not at the passengers seated behind him. There is also a female attendant who left the bus at an earlier stop, but the young woman remembers nothing. Then he searches for the male names on the listing. There are nine of them. The seventh name on the list is a man named Amos Posner in Amagansett. The name means nothing to him.

He decides to visit the area, books a rental car and a motel room for one night. He opts not to call anyone in advance, but to take his chance that some of the people will be available. Heidi has been gone for nearly six weeks, and there is no word, sign, or evidence that she was ever there. He has paid her rent for the past two months. He learns that her parents in Austria have already been informed of her disappearance by the NYPD, but a short answer in good English says they are not planning to come at this time. A third party signs the reply. The response confuses him. He wonders what kind of people they are, and immediately speculates what kind of relationship they had for them to take such a distant approach. Most families would have arrived on the first available flight. Was it a Muslim or an Austrian cultural thing, or something else? His confusion grows apace with his fear. He increases the dosage of the anxiety meds he's taken for several years. He needs a clear rational mind if he has any chance of finding out anything more.

He sits on the bed in his East Hampton motel room with the police summary he obtained from his FOIA filing. Amos Posner is one of only three people on the bus who live in the town of East Hampton. All of the names came up on Google. One was an eighty-year-old former staff member of *The New Yorker* magazine, but the man was clearly barely coherent when Henry called.

Posner's Google listing was brief. He had been involved in international trade for years with a large firm, but suddenly lost his position two years before. He is married and lives in Amagansett.

Henry calls and after four rings expects an answering machine to pick up, but the dial tone continues. The man must be away, or has turned off his machine. He marks the space next to Posner's name for follow-up after noting the time of his call.

The final name is a man named Welbrook who also lives in Amagansett. A number of Google references indicate a position in entertainment law. He answers on the first ring.

"Well, I already told the police that I didn't remember her. It's been a while since the day they said she disappeared, and I go back and forth to the city at least once a week, sometimes more often."

Henry has introduced himself as a doctor and a friend of the missing woman. The doctor part always helps. There is still respect in society for the profession, although far from where it was when he was a kid. Today's icons are more likely to be athletes, investment bankers, or maybe international specialists like that guy Posner.

"Could I stop by and show you some other pictures of Heidi? They're much better than the fax copy the police showed you. I promise you it won't take much time and it might jog your memory."

"As long as you make it quick," says Welbrook and gives directions from the motel. Henry has already picked up an area map at the front desk provided by a local real estate broker.

He traces the route on the map with his pen, stands and reaches for the envelope with the three color photos. The bottom one was taken on their Bermuda trip. She's standing on the beach and squinting slightly into a bright sun. A calm ocean lies in the background. She's wearing the new pink-and-white dress.

Welbrook's house is less than ten minutes away, and lies at the end of a stretch of road dominated by large modern homes with decks that face the ocean. Many seem to have enclosed pool areas. Henry realizes there is great opulence here, and that most of these houses have ocean views. A vintage Mercedes sedan is parked in a cutout just off the driveway.

"Yes. Now I remember her. It's the dress. Pink and white. It was sorta cut low on top, if you know what I mean."

John Welbrook is a good-looking man in his early forties with curly blond hair. Henry feels an immediate and absurd sense of jealousy as soon as the man opens the door. Welbrook has the looks and obvious self-confidence to have attracted Heidi, and from his memory of her dress, she would have attracted him as well.

They stand in the wide hallway. Henry's attention is drawn to the walls, which are decorated with photos of various celebrities from the theatre, sports, and politics. Welbrook notes his interest and claims they are all clients of his firm that specializes in entertainment law. Stern turns his attention back to a short flight of stairs that rise from the hallway and empties into a large room with a vaulted ceiling. He follows Welbrook up the stairs, but is not invited to sit.

"So do you remember anything else about her?"

"When I spoke to the police I wasn't sure I remembered her from the faxed picture, but the color photo and that dress—it's not easy to forget that dress."

"Did you talk to her? Did she happen to say anything?"

"Actually, I was going to the rest room. That's in the back of the bus. She was sitting near the back and stopped me and asked how to get to the beach from the East Hampton stop. I probably told her she'd have to take a cab. That's when she asked me if I could drive her.

"Told her no. Even though I live in Amagansett, told her I was getting off in East Hampton village. That's where I parked my car. Said I had things to do. Didn't have the time to drive her to the beach. Nor the particular interest."

Henry lets the words slide past him, and looks around the room.

"Nice house," Henry says.

"We like it," answers Welbrook.

"Oh, you're married," says Henry.

"Not at the moment," answers Welbrook, and slips away a tiny laugh.

Henry takes a few steps towards a floor-to-ceiling glass window and looks out.

"That's quite a view."

"Sure. Most houses anywhere this close to the beach usually have some ocean view. It's what people pay top dollar for."

Henry takes a chance and decides to see if Posner's home without first calling since the drive is only minutes away. Welbrook's house is clearly larger and closer to the beach than Posner's, but both houses do indeed seem to have an ocean view. Henry's rented Chevy climbs the driveway and stops behind a parked Lexus.

Without an entry bell he raps with the brass knocker that guards the door. There is no response for at least thirty seconds, and he's just about to leave when he hears a voice from inside.

"Who is it? I'll be there in a minute."

The voice is clear and slightly faint, almost tired, Henry thinks, before he raps again, more briefly this time, and announces himself as a doctor friend of Heidi, whom he describes as the missing woman from the bus. The door opens. He apologizes for the unannounced nature of his visit and watches as Posner releases the door even wider as an unspoken invitation to enter. He follows Posner up the stairs to a living area with its own ocean views. He sees the twin green sofas, set around the art deco coffee table, and imagines that Heidi might have been here, just as she might have been in Welbrook's home, or one like it. He inhales the affluence of the room. Doctors may be paid well by comparison to other work, but there is no way he can ever see affording such luxury. There is art on the walls, probably original prints. Some of the images are familiar: a Picasso Don Quixote and a full-sized Rauschenberg share space on the far wall. From what he's read on Google, Posner has not worked for a few years, yet his art collection seems significant enough, and the house is quite grand by Henry's standards even if slightly more modest than Welbrook's.

Further introductions are brief. Posner clearly prefers that he not be there, but Henry is now used to this attitude after his time with Welbrook.

"Do you remember this woman?" he asks when the preliminaries are over.

Posner looks briefly at the photo Henry presents. Almost too briefly, Henry thinks, but he sees Posner clearly stare at the image with the pink-and-white dress.

"Oh, that's definitely her," he says, echoing Welbrook's recollection.

As with Welbrook, Henry has prepared himself for some confession of sorts, an act of contrition, and an acknowledgment that the man had some involvement with Heidi, but there is nothing. In this regard, Posner behaves much the same as Welbrook. He relates his recollection of their brief bus conversation. Heidi appears to have asked both men for a ride to the beach. He sighs and wonders whom else she spoke to after she left the bus. Conversation then stalls. Henry stands and walks toward the steps. He moves down the stairs without incident, stands beside the front door, turns, and asks, "Would you mind if I called on you again? There may be something else you might remember."

Posner doesn't answer. He merely shrugs his shoulders a moment before the door clicks shut.

# CHAPTER 5

Peter Wisdom watches the lazy fly ball float toward his son Kevin in right field. Kevin moves to his left, hesitates as he squints into the late afternoon sun, wavers for a moment as he surely loses sight of the ball, then lunges to the side and stabs it inches above the ground. The gathering of parents and friends applaud the effort.

Wisdom joins in, then turns around, faces the setting orange ball, and thinks again of the missing woman. She has become hard to forget. Perhaps the sun has been in his eyes too long. He's missing something and realizes it's become personal. He admits that the woman holds some physical attraction for him.

He remembers an old film where a police detective investigates the suspected murder of a beautiful woman and becomes obsessed with her portrait, until events change and she turns up alive. In this case, the missing woman doctor named Heidi Kashani has not turned up, yet Wisdom feels an uncontrolled obsession beginning to grow. Perhaps that is why he carries the color photo of her in the pink-and-white dress that Stern gave him. There is an exotic sexuality in her eyes, and from the way Stern describes her, he can understand Stern's own obsession. Moreover he can understand why other men might easily become attracted.

He notes that he should ask NYPD for a detailed check on Stern, and particularly his whereabouts on the day the woman disappeared. Obsession can beget violence. He has seen it too often. Still, there is no evidence of a crime, much less a death. Wisdom knows they would need considerable circumstantial evidence in the absence of physical proof. All the more reason for him to inquire about the whereabouts of Dr. Henry Stern on a chilly day this past May. Since so many capital crimes involve people who know each other, this is as good a place to start as anywhere else. He knows that the NYPD won't be too happy. If someone goes missing outside of the city, then another jurisdiction has the problem, but in the end they'll still help out.

He becomes lost in thought as the teams change sides. Since early in the case he's assumed that the woman is dead. It might not even have been murder. She might have become lost in the woods and fallen into a sinkhole. All he knows is that she disappeared after leaving the bus in East Hampton, and apparently after trying to induce two separate men to drive her to the beach. She might even have gone back to Austria as some of his colleagues at County have suggested, although there is no record of her being on any scheduled flight. The fact that her parents have not offered to come to America puzzles him. The reasonable conclusion is that they know where she is, but they neither offer nor ask for help from the police.

By all accounts the woman was reasonably content at work and had a rather active social life, especially with Henry Stern. Yes, he tells himself, we'll start with a closer look at Dr. Stern. If he was involved in Heidi's disappearance, his behavior since then would give him an opportunity to deflect suspicion. Stern's actions in providing the photos and insisting on interviewing other passengers all represent the expected activity of a concerned boyfriend, except that Wisdom could hear an obsession in the man's voice that gives him pause. His contacts at NYPD will give it all a good look. No one has yet suggested that they call in the FBI. Hell. There isn't even any evidence of a kidnapping.

He looks up just in time to see his son swinging a bat as he moves into the on-deck area. There is only an inning to go and he wants to watch the whole game. In the summer he never knows how many

Little League games he'll get to. You never stop being on the job even when you're off the clock.

The next morning Detective Wisdom sits at his desk, yawns, and reaches for the Starbuck's iced cappuccino. It's Thursday, a late-June Thursday, and every Thursday he promises himself a stop at the East Hampton Starbuck's even though it's a bit out of the way. He's already savored the last few crumbs of the bran muffin. He flips open his notebook and rereads his neat printed summary of what he needs to do that day. For the moment he ignores the files that lie on the corner of his desk regarding detailed follow-up of police-related activities; a break-in and robbery at an expensive house in East Hampton, a possible hate crime assault of a local Hispanic landscaper in the Springs, and a fight outside a bar in Montauk in the early morning of the past Saturday. Things will be getting worse. The season has just begun. There will be fights, robberies, even the rare possibility of a murder. There will likely be more overtime, although he would prefer there wasn't. He's already missed two of his son's Little League games.

He closes the pad and sighs. Something gnaws at him. The missing woman from New York. He hasn't made any progress. Then a small kernel of an idea grows. He picks up the phone and dials the extension of the department's tech specialist.

After two rings, Ray Baxter picks up.

"Ray. Peter Wisdom. Can you please clarify something for me? If someone used a two or three-year-old Verizon wireless cell phone six weeks ago, can you still tell me where the call was made from? Sorry, but we don't have the phone. I'd rather ask you first than depend on Verizon. I'll talk to them when we know more." Wisdom fills in more of the details and leaves the rest to the resident techie.

Ray calls back the next morning.

"Sorry it took so long, but I wanted to check something with the

Feds before getting back. You were right to ask. The technology changes so fast these days that something new could turn up tomorrow. Anyway, the story is this: If the woman's phone was a few years old, it probably didn't have one of the new embedded chips. If she did, the new tracking systems would enable Verizon to pinpoint the source of the call to within fifty feet or less. Assuming she didn't have the chip, and the call was made a few months ago, the best they could do would be to determine that the call was transmitted through a local tower. In this case it was probably in Amagansett."

"Remind me. Where's the tower?" asks Wisdom, oblivious to his admission that he didn't remember exactly where, although he'd knew about the construction several years before.

Ray gives the location. It's a quasi-industrial area away from the larger summer homes. The rich don't want a tall radio tower in their backyard.

"What's the area range that it covers?" asks Wisdom.

"That's the problem," said Ray. "It's a pretty big area. Look at it as a pie shape with a diameter of two to three miles. Around here that especially covers a lot of space with water views. You did say the call came from a house with water views, didn't you?"

Wisdom sighs and breathes faint curses into the receiver. Ray doesn't need to repeat the question.

"As long as the Feds aren't involved there's not usually a problem and city hasn't suggested calling them in as yet. Nor should we or County. So far there's absolutely no hint of a kidnapping. Damn!"

Chief Ferris manages to get all but the last few words out before a drop of yolk from his fried egg breakfast sandwich leaks onto his shirt. He looks down, wets his handkerchief with a daub from his tongue, and blots the spot as he shakes his head.

"Lucky I always keep extra shirts in the office closet, but first let's see how it dries."

He's called Wisdom into his office on a cool August day to fill him in on the "Heidi case" as they called it in the office. He doesn't often get so involved in a case, but Wisdom is happy for the input. The chief has been around and knows the score. He pulls a folder up from his clean desk and reads from the combined NYPD and town reports.

"After nearly three months of waiting, nothing's turned up. When she disappeared, she had over thirty thousand dollars in her bank account at Chase, and more to the point there weren't any recent major cash withdrawals. The last one was the day before she took the bus and that was only for a hundred. All of the last checks she wrote were for normal commercial expenses like rent, Con Edison, Verizon, and the Food Emporium. She has one credit card, a Chase Visa. Not much there except for some department store clothing purchases. Again nothing since she went missing. Certainly no purchase of airline or railroad tickets.

"They haven't heard anymore from her parents in Europe, which boggles the mind, nor have they opted to call in the Feds. What they have done is follow an idea you had to check out Dr. Stern more closely. Initially they thought it was far-fetched. After all he was the one who first reported her missing. They had a strong emotional relationship and he brought in the cell phone message where she said she was in some nice house out here with a water view."

"We know all that," says Wisdom. "Did they find anything?"

"More than a little. First thing is that Stern can't confirm an alibi for that day. Says he wasn't on call on the day she disappeared. Says he rented a car and drove upstate to the area where he grew up, had a bite at some diner and came back late afternoon. Didn't talk to anyone who would remember him, didn't use a credit card for anything. Nada."

"So what's wrong with the picture?"

"The mileage to start with. Several weeks later he rented another car also from the same Avis East Side pick-up location. You'll remember that's when he came out here with the FOIA list and spoke to some people from the bus. The mileage on the day he came out here was almost the same as the time when he claimed he went upstate."

"Meaning he could have been here and not upstate on the day she disappeared. Meaning he could have followed her out to East Hampton and trailed her from the bus stop. But what about the cell phone call he got from her? Wouldn't his phone have shown that he was out here when he received the call?"

"Claims he forgot the phone that day. Says he was pissed that she didn't want him to come along and accidentally left it back in his apartment and only got her message when he got home."

"That sounds lame. He's a doctor for chrissakes. He needs to be available twenty-four seven."

"Says he did have his pager but had no messages."

"Anything else?"

"NYPD also says they made some discreet inquiries about the relationship between the two of them. Seems they were getting it off pretty regularly, but she wasn't doing it only with him. She was pretty accommodating to anyone on the staff who showed any interest. So much so they had some fights that weren't so private, but they haven't hit him yet with any of this."

"Jesus!" Wisdom shakes his head sideways in a universal sign of disapproval. "So are we still involved at all?"

"Not directly, but there are two more things you should know about. When New York was talking to Stern, he volunteered that he had a feeling that either of two guys from the bus probably knew more than they were letting on. They'd like us to talk to them again. It's Welbrook and Posner. Before you say anything, I know you already spoke to both of them and they were clean, but we'd be doing the city boys a favor, and I like it when they owe us. And before you see them, do some research on their backgrounds. If by any chance they're lying to us, I want to know enough so we can catch them in it. I spoke to County and they're with us on this."

The report on Wisdom's meetings with Posner and Welbrook rests in a growing folder he holds in his lap. Posner remains a very long shot possible suspect in Heidi's disappearance based solely on the chance bus meeting, although Wisdom has no reason to put much faith in this theory. He doesn't need to find the interview report with Welbrook to remember that particular exchange.

Benjamin Welbrook agreed to meet with Wisdom on short notice. His house is larger than Posner's and has more panoramic ocean views, but both houses exude a level of wealth found with some prevalence throughout the area. Wisdom's summary describes Welbrook as a very poised middle-aged individual involved in entertainment law. He dresses in simple, yet elegant clothing; white linen pants and a blue designer shirt with the sleeves rolled to the elbows. He uses the house in Amagansett to entertain clients and for weekend getaways with his partner whom Wisdom meets during the meeting.

Welbrook introduces his partner as Steven Hoyle. Hoyle has dark hair and wears a tee shirt and worn jeans with a large hole over one knee. He appears slightly younger than Welbrook and is an editorial associate for a major publishing firm. They offer coffee and sit on the opposite couch from Wisdom. Welbrook drapes an arm around Hoyle's shoulder, which he periodically massages. The effect is obvious. Wisdom has no interest in the man's sexual orientation except that it minimizes Welbrook's possible interest in Heidi Kashani, although that doesn't mean elimination. Welbrook still remains a minor focus, but is now in the second tier, if such a distinction is possible.

In Wisdom's opinion Dr. Stern is still front and center the most likely to be involved. All this flashes through Wisdom's mind in seconds, but the chief doesn't seem to notice any delay in his answer.

"Let me think about how to approach this. Stern is a more likely suspect that these other two. Sounds like he's just trying to throw us off. Did the city cops happen to mention whether Stern did anything to indicate that he felt he was a possible suspect?"

"Nothing they picked up on. But if I wanted to off my girlfriend, one good way to cover up might be to report her missing and then try to steer the blame to someone else. That's if I had a girlfriend I wanted to disappear, which I don't, and if I had one that looked like Heidi, I absolutely wouldn't."

Wisdom stands and sighs in one motion, almost as if his body was controlled by some outside puppeteer. He starts to walk toward the door then stops and turns sharply.

"You said there were two more things. Another go-round with these two dudes is one. What's the other?"

Ferris smiles into his nearly empty coffee cup.

"The hospital got a call. Seems Heidi has a sister and she'll be arriving in the city in a week and plans on visiting us the following Tuesday."

Wisdom glances at the wall calendar, which is distributed by a local nonprofit. Smack in the middle of the last week in August, as busy a week as they're likely to get all summer.

"The Austrian Consulate in the city has asked that she be given the full treatment. Actually the call to the hospital came from State. The sister's a special assistant to some UN bigwig in Geneva. And if you're at all curious why I'm so interested in this case, then you can blame the State Department. Enjoy your weekend."

# CHAPTER 6

Brigid Kashani sits on the chair in Ferris's office. She is flanked on one side by a man from the Austrian Consulate who introduces himself as Bernd Weis. He's dressed all in charcoal gray except for a dazzling white shirt that is slashed by a tie that matches his suit color. Sergeant Rick Bennett, who runs the squad of seven detectives on the town force and is Wisdom's boss, sits on her other side facing Wisdom and Ferris. Lieutenant Walker might otherwise have taken the chief's place, but international embassy visitors call for a certain protocol.

Bennett's hair is starting to gray and his belly just begins to push against a wrinkled shirt bunched at his gut, but his appearance is deceptive. His mind is both fertile and agile, always on the alert to ambush a contradiction in a story. After twenty years on the job, he's become a very good cop. Bennett actually started with the department in East Hampton Village as a teenage summer traffic control officer—what the locals still call "a sand cop"—writing parking tickets. Today he's arguably one of the best general detectives in the whole county and the town is lucky that he never left.

Wisdom looks again at Brigid while Ferris relays soft drink requests on the phone to his secretary. Brigid looks very much like Heidi down to the same short black helmet of hair Wisdom memorized from the photo; a slightly larger than normal nose, full lips, wide dark eyes and a light-brown Middle Eastern coloring. There is one major obvious difference. Brigid Kashani wears a business suit over a blouse buttoned to her neck. There is no hint at sexuality either in her choice of clothing or her makeup, which are both understated and practical. Yet when he looks only at her eyes, Wisdom sees a hint of the veiled sensuality that Stern and presumably others have seen in Heidi.

Soft drinks arrive at the same time as a written message for Ferris that causes him to make excuses and exit, leaving Wisdom and Bennett to run the meeting. Bennett winks at Wisdom. It's an old game they've played before to keep the chief out of the details.

She begins to speak. Wisdom hears a German accent for sure, but it sounds as much British as German. Presumably she'd learned her English from a Brit. There's also the absence of any of the rough throaty edges usually associated with German. Bennett comments on this and she explains that years in the French speaking part of Switzerland together with a year and a half of graduate school in Boston has softened her Austrian inflection.

"I only saw the message about Heidi last weekend when I went back to Vienna. My father never saw it, and if he had, he wouldn't have answered. It was my aunt who lives with my parents who saw the message and sent the answer, because for both of my parents, Heidi no longer exists. It's not even as though she had died. It's as if she'd never existed."

Bennett mirrors Wisdom's look of bewilderment. Weis sits as before, if anything he is more stoic and Wisdom wonders if a test of his diplomatic skill is whether he can absorb such news without as much as a quiver of facial expression. Brigid, however, doesn't miss Wisdom's reaction. She is ready to go on.

"I needed to be in New York anyway, so I decided to come directly to see the authorities rather than handle it long distance. Let me say that I do acknowledge that Heidi exists, but I don't really care whether she's alive or dead."

Her words hang in the air. Everyone waits for the explanation—the complete version—there is nothing else to say.

Even Weis moves perceptibly forward to the edge of his seat. He doesn't have long to wait.

"Let me tell you a story," she says, her hands clasped together demurely in her lap, as if in church.

"I am three years older than Heidi. We were both born in a suburb of Tehran. My Persian name was Behjat. Hers was Hediyeh. After we moved to Vienna, our parents changed the first names to conform to local customs, so hers converted into Heidi and mine became Brigid. We moved in the last days of the shah. My father had already arranged for money to be sent out of the country so we were quite comfortable after we arrived in Austria. We had a fine house, went to the best schools, learned to ski in the winter and sail in the summer. Heidi wanted to study medicine and I was interested in economics and international affairs. We both did college and graduate work in Switzerland.

"Soon after I started with the UN in Geneva, I met a young French Jewish lawyer who worked in the same agency. We fell in love and got engaged. We were to be married the next summer. That Christmas I invited him home to Vienna to meet my parents and Heidi."

She stops abruptly, takes a long swallow from a cup of Sprite, and looks up at Wisdom.

"Can one smoke here?" she asks.

Wisdom might have denied her, but now just waves his hand and reaches for a battered brass beaker from the top of a bookcase where it still rests despite an official ban on smoking. Bennett gives a perceptible tilt of his head in agreement. She takes a cigarette from a blue packet within her small bag and lights up with a silver-colored lighter. In a moment the air fills with an acrid grayish-blue cloud. Wisdom absently wonders whether Bennett who has recently again given up smoking is crawling inside his skin. She takes another puff then grinds the butt into the brass.

"Take your time," Bennett offers, possibly sensing that the next part will be more difficult.

"Thank you. Two days after we'd arrived back in Vienna, my mother and I were looking for some old photo albums and tried an unused storage room. That's where we found them. Heidi and Philippe were half naked and having sex. Philippe was shocked and embarrassed, but all she did was half turn around and smile. I'll never forget that smile. It was like she was saying 'so what!'

"They left the house together minutes later and we never saw either of them again. That night my father said that if we were all back in Iran, under Sharia or Islamic law, the Koran would call for her to be stoned to death and her family forever held in contempt by the local community. Well, we weren't back in Iran, but since then my parents acted as if she had brought dishonor to our household. They pronounced her a nonperson and just behaved as if she never existed. I never saw Philippe again. He quit the agency, and I later heard he died in an automobile accident in Bavaria. It was partly my mistake in getting involved with such a weak person, but Heidi was in a way already crazy, only we didn't see it."

She stops, pulls another cigarette from her bag, and holds it up. Wisdom signals his agreement and she repeats the earlier ritual of two puffs before extinction. She seems to possess incredible self-control, he thinks, to be able to handle all this with strangers. He shifts in his seat and leans forward.

"When she was only sixteen, I found out that she already had sex with a neighbor's son. After I challenged her with this, she only laughed and said she planned to do it next with his father. I never confronted her again, but over the next few years, bits and pieces of what she did and what she thought came out. I learned that it was Jewish men she went after. She was determined to prove herself better, determined to show them she was in control. And she found she could use sex as a way to get the power.

"I wasn't sure why she felt this way unless she got it from our father who blamed the Jews for displacing us years ago. But then he also blamed the other Arab states, the Americans, and the Communists. Why she singled out the Jews I'll never know."

The words hang in the air like wood smoke. Bennett clears his throat. Weis bends to the side and whispers to her as she reaches for another cigarette. She hands one to Weis and they both smoke. Wisdom thinks that Chief Ferris was very shortly going to be pissed bigtime at the invasive tobacco smell in his office. This time, as if to reinforce his thoughts, she keeps the cigarette alive past a few drags, although Wisdom thinks she'd be better off with a glass of vodka. He certainly would.

"When was the last time you heard from her?" asks Bennett. "Was it the night she left your parent's home in Vienna?"

"No. About two years ago I got a very short note from her. Said she had just come to the States for her residency. That's all. No apologies. No suggestions we meet. No matter what happened or what my parents feel or I feel, she's still my sister. I need to end this. I need closure. Please find out what happened to her."

No one speaks. The room is quiet except for the distant hum of an air conditioner.

"Do you know if a man might be involved? Probably a Jewish man. It would make some sense if there was."

Wisdom catches Bennett's eye without difficulty and tilts his head perceptibly.

"The police are pursuing some possibilities," Bennett says, "But there isn't anything concrete at this time."

She stares ahead and jams the cigarette out. Then for a brief moment she looks like she was going to cry, but the moment passes and she's back in control. She leans toward Weis and mumbles something in German. Wisdom looks at Bennett who shakes his head sideways. Weis asks if they're done.

"For now." Wisdom and Bennett both answer. Weis rises and takes Brigid's arm to help her stand, but she eases her arm free. *This is one tough lady,* Wisdom thinks.

"Can we reach you if we need to speak again?" he asks.

"That won't be a problem," she says. "I'll be staying at the guest-house of one of the Washington Embassy people for a few days. It's actually very close to here. My luggage is in Herr Weis's car. I also plan to take a leave of absence from work for as much as a few months and rent a place in the area. I understand it will be easy to do after your Labor Day weekend. The senior people in Geneva have already approved the idea. I need to find out what happened and I think the answer is out here somewhere. If you need me, Herr Weis will have my number and address."

Then she points to the photo of Heidi that rests atop the open file. "May I have a copy of that?"

Wisdom is quick to answer. "Yes. We have copies," and he hands her the picture.

Weis produces a card that seems to appear from up his sleeve and passes it to Wisdom. They all shake hands. Wisdom is surprised that Brigid's feels incredibly warm for someone with such a controlled exterior. The two Austrians walk a few steps toward the door that Bennett holds open. Weis waits for Brigid to pass ahead when she stops and faces Wisdom.

"Do you think she's still alive?" she asks. He feels her eyes bore right through him.

Before he can answer, she turns and walks through the door with Weis in pursuit. Wisdom watches them disappear down the hall through the opaque glass on the top half of the door.

"So what do you think?" Wisdom asks after they reassume their seats.

Bennett pulls his chair closer to Wisdom despite the fact that they're alone.

"I think we just found someone who had a real reason to make our friend Heidi disappear. Lucky for her she wasn't in town back in early May. But we'll check that out just to be sure. By the way. Posner and Stern are both Jewish, aren't they?"

Wisdom nods then leaves to find and update Chief Ferris while Bennett returns to his routine, which includes updating NYPD, whose interest had fallen from curiosity to nonexistent in the past few months. As far as he can tell, he's the only one in law enforcement who has the slightest interest in finding out about what happened to Heidi Kashani. There is Bennett, of course, but his interest at this point seems more academic than anything else. Maybe he thinks it's all just a waste of everyone's time. And the chief? Well, his top priority is not to discover a body hidden away somewhere in tourist season. Soon after the issue was first raised, Wisdom and Chief Ferris briefed two town councilmen and the supervisor about the case and left the elected officials with the assurances that, "If something bad happened to the young woman, it couldn't have been in our town."

Wisdom is for all intent and purposes on his own. So be it, he thinks.

# CHAPTER 7

Ten days have gone by since the first meeting with Brigid. Summer is now almost officially over and nothing about the missing New York female doctor has surfaced to disturb the Town Board. Then out of nowhere, Brigid calls to advise Wisdom she's rented a house in Montauk for the next two months.

"It's on the Old Montauk Highway and looks out over the ocean. I've never lived in such a place before."

Wisdom tells her he hopes she'll find some peace and comfort and was about to hang up when she says she has an idea she needs to speak to him about. She says it's important.

He reluctantly agrees to meet with her later that afternoon, but not before repeating to her what Bennett said at their initial meeting,

"You realize that this is still a local investigation. So far there's no basis for calling in the County on suspicion of a major crime. And as far as NYPD, the New York City Police, well, they're just happy she didn't disappear in the city."

"Yes, I know all this," she says almost too quickly, "But I am living here for now and I want to do something. I need to talk to someone, certainly not the FBI or the New York City Police. It's far easier to talk to someone I've already met who's also out here. Can't I just do that?"

At five thirty that afternoon Wisdom pulls his unmarked blue Ford Crown Vic into an empty driveway that descends slightly from Old Montauk Highway. The driveway curves around to behind the house where he assumes she parks, but he stops and parks just feet from the front door. He sighs with a controlled weariness and glances again through the case file that rests on the empty passenger seat. He stares one last time at the photo of Heidi. He has gotten to know her face well over the past several months, but until meeting her sister he never really began to have a sense of the person.

The house is low and wrapped with horizontal slices of worn cedar planks that glisten with flashes of silver in the late afternoon sun. From the driveway with the curtains open he looks through the large picture window that exposes a stark interior. He sees an even larger picture window at the back of the room that guards a rear deck cantilevered out from the cliff it had been built into. Specks of white foam fly out from above the ocean beyond. From experience he knows that there is likely another floor downstairs that isn't visible from the outside. All in all, quite a house.

He walks from the car to the front door. As he waits for a reply to his knock, he hears the rhythm of rolling surf some hundred feet below interspersed with the shriek from a circling bird.

"Come in. The door is open."

It's Brigid's voice. He prefers that she open the door, but there's no further sound so he pushes forward and the wood slides silently open. He moves into the house and stands a few feet from the door. Everything is in white; the walls, furniture, and rugs all bring a dazzling starkness that competes favorably with the still visibly robust sunlight.

"Hello," he calls out into the silence. He waits. It's probably no more than thirty seconds, yet seems longer, until he hears a rustle of movement to the side. He turns to the right barely in time to catch a flash of a minidress with pink-and-white polka dots.

"What do you think?" she says and spins onto a short pirouette.

Wisdom draws in his breath. She is no longer Brigid, but has transformed herself into Heidi. He feels he's seeing a ghost. She has used the photo in the police files to copy her sister's look. The dress is tight and cut low over her breasts. He hasn't a clue how she managed to get so similar a dress in such a short a time. She wears hoop earrings and a hint of color seems to swell her lips. There is barely a touch of other makeup. She stands scarcely five feet away and he realizes this is what Heidi's boyfriend, the doctor, and obviously others have seen; a voluptuous woman with a dark riveting stare that has the capacity to instantly arouse.

That's the moment when he remembers the name of the old film he'd thought about over the past weeks. It was called *Laura.* The protagonist is a cop investigating the murder of a woman whose face had been obliterated by a shotgun blast. The cop sits in the dead woman's apartment trying to make sense of her death while a portrait of the slain woman, which hangs in the room, becomes a visible companion. The woman is beautiful and the cop can't help but stare wistfully at the waste her death has brought, while he imagines what it might have been like to know her. Then the door opens and the woman appears, still alive and even more attractive than the painted image. Another woman had been killed by accident and the cop is suddenly confronted with the live object of his fantasies.

This is how Wisdom feels. He is looking at Brigid, but seeing Heidi. Seeing her as all the others may have seen her, and in a moment as clear as fall air, he's pretty sure he knows why she's asked him here and what this is all about.

Two days later Chief Ferris can only promise Wisdom a short meeting, but it turns out he miscalculates. The *New York Times* is doing one of its endless annual pieces on life in the Hamptons, or as one reporter had asked the previous year, "Other than DWIs, do you get any serious crimes here after Labor Day?" But this interview will have to wait. That morning's half-finished cappuccino cup rests on the corner of the gray steel desk dangerously close to Wisdom's loafers. He checks his watch, swings his legs off the desk, and grunts silently at the minor effort. He gathers the Heidi file in one hand, snatches the cappuccino in the other, and moves quickly down the corridor toward the chief's office.

Wisdom takes nearly ten minutes to tell his story and then does it again when they are joined by the town attorney, and then for a third time when Sergeant Bennett arrives. They discuss whether it's still too early to call in County's major-crimes people. In the end, they compromise on the plan to have Bennett call his counterpart at County and fill him in on where they stand as of as now. Then they go round and round regarding the strategy Wisdom has presented and its pitfalls, particularly entrapment.

"It's all her idea. Brigid's," he explains. "But I think it's worth trying. She feels that since she looks so much like her sister, if she appears suddenly in front of any possible suspects, it might trigger a shock that could produce some worthwhile reaction. We have nothing to lose if we're careful about the entrapment issue and we could have a wire available to avoid a problem."

"Shock and awe," mumbles Bennett. His voice fills a momentary lull before the town attorney infuriates Wisdom when he asks him to review the plan still again.

Wisdom dutifully repeats his earlier narration of his visit to Brigid's rented house in Montauk. He describes how she looked much like her missing sister whose photo has previously been shared with all participants. But this time the review of the meeting with Brigid produces an unusual, more personal effect. His thoughts wander even as he speaks about her plan. It is as if his brain separates the area that controls his mechanically delivered speech that deals with a strategy from another, more distant part of his mind that replays a more private memory about her effect on him on that afternoon.

She leads him into the whitewashed living space and waits until he sits on the light beige leather sofa. The wide planked floors are bleached and coated with a clear dull finish. The walls are bare, except for one abstract oil composed of slashes of black, gray, and the ubiquitous white. A heavy glass ashtray rests on a white painted rattan coffee table that fronts the sofa.

"Would you like something to drink? Some wine?" she asks. "I'm having a nice Chardonnay from here on Long Island. From a vineyard called Wolffer Estate. Do you know it?"

"Yes, it's got a good reputation, and thanks, but I'll pass for now."

As he speaks, she reaches down to an end table and lifts a half-filled glass to her mouth. After she sips he sees a wet film spread across her lips. He feels a flush rising in his face.

"I imagine that I don't need your permission to smoke in my own house, but do you mind?"

"No," he says although something actually makes him want to smoke himself even though he hasn't had an urge for several years.

He watches her draw a cigarette from a packet of Gauloises and light the end with a blue flame. She sits next to him with one arm on the back edge of the sofa barely inches from his shoulder while she holds the cigarette in her free hand. He notices that she wears no jewelry and that her nails are clipped short and without polish. She crosses one leg over the other so that the already short skirt rides up her thigh.

It is all so obvious and he tells her so then adds, "So what's this all about? Why the show?"

She smiles. A good smile. He hadn't seen her smile before. She uncrosses her legs, sits up straight and smoothes her skirt.

"I look like her. We both know I do. You've seen her photo. When we were still in our teens we used to dress up when our parents were out. We'd try on sexy things and compete with each other. And this is how she might have looked and acted. I know. I've seen her do it before. I mean attracting men. What do you think? Is this an attractive look?"

She was playing him. They both know it and he smiles back at her, but there is something else going on, at least for Wisdom. It is all about sexuality. Her sexuality. He can't help himself. His eyes are riveted on her face and body. He imagines the full lips under his. His mind peels away the top of her dress and sees her breasts, heavy with brown nipples, then lifts away the thong underwear and finds a mass of dark moist curls spread across the vee between her legs. All this passes in the seconds she takes to flick an ash from the end of her cigarette. It is in his mind, even more so after hearing firsthand about Heidi. So this is the look that drove her boyfriend and others crazy with lust. Maybe the same look that tipped the balance of safety against her. He barely notices when Brigid excuses herself and disappears into another room, but he's thankful. If he had to stand the bulge in his pants would have been all too obvious.

She comes back a few minutes later looking as she had the day they'd first met at the department. She's exchanged the dress for a white blouse buttoned to the edge of her neck, dark pants, a green cardigan sweater, and simple black flats. The transformation back is complete. She is once again the nice-looking thirty-something career woman from Europe who works for the UN. There is no hint of the overt sexuality he'd witnessed minutes before.

"You've changed." He knows the words are unnecessary, but he really wants to ask why.

"I had to. I felt too much like her. I felt almost—dirty."

Wisdom doesn't answer and feels embarrassed at his earlier thoughts. They spend the next twenty minutes going over her ideas and his reservations, and in the end he promises to see if he can sell the idea. He leaves the house as the last fingers of sunlight stretch across the driveway. He starts to drive away and finds himself laboring under a growing cloud of guilt about why he wishes she hadn't changed out of the pink-and-white dress.

✦ ✦ ✦

The police and attorneys agree it isn't entrapment if she doesn't say anything more than a hello. It's agreed that safety requires Wisdom accompany her to meetings with Posner and Welbrook even though NYPD's investigation has confirmed Wisdom's view that that Welbrook's openly gay and would likely have had no obvious interest in being involved with Heidi. Still, he was a long shot possibility and at some point should be confronted, but not at first. That honor will belong to Posner and Stern. They will need to separately talk to NYPD about the doctor boyfriend, but Bennett is confident the city cops will go along. The plan is to try for meetings within the next week. Wisdom will call to set up appointments. The whole meeting lasts just over an hour. Wisdom goes back to his office and pulls out phone numbers for Welbrook and Posner. Then he stares at the phone and considers what he might say.

# CHAPTER 8

Amos Posner is virtually happy living in the metaphysical fog that allows him to speculate that Heidi's body will never be found. There have been no more police visits or that of the doctor boyfriend from Manhattan. On top of that nothing has surfaced regarding the federal investigation into his activities except the ongoing knowledge that with every month that passes, the statute of limitations affords less time for the Justice Department to proceed against him. His mind gradually accepts the current status and the inevitability of living with thoughts of Heidi throughout his life.

He remembers a Woody Allen film, *Crimes and Misdemeanors,* where a straying husband arranges for the murder of his mistress when she threatens to expose him. Sometime after her death, when the investigation has passed and his innocence is unquestioned, he basks in the realization that he has gotten away with a crime. Posner can only bide his time. What has it been? Almost five months.

Time has not healed the pain as much as he thought it would after the first few months. A distance between Sara and him remains, but he senses some very gradual improvement although he continues to sleep on the sofa bed when he's in the city. He no longer asks if she plans to spend time in Amagansett and she never mentions it. His small attempts at what for him are unaccustomed displays of general household assistance acknowledge he's somehow been at fault; he vacuums, empties the dishwasher, or scrubs the bathrooms. They begin to speak with some regularity, but limit their dialogue to commonplace matters; the dishwasher's chronic need for repair, whether they should repaint the living room, a visit to the dentist, or the state of federal and local politics. But they do speak, which is a major advance. And he still disappears with regularity, as if on a schedule, for several days at a time back to Amagansett and to the beaches and ocean he loves so much. Time helps. His melancholy begins to ebb and he discovers that he can function in and around the house without the constant reminder of the tragedy that occurred. Yet he is often lonely and another fear takes hold; at times when he's at the beach house and tries to reach her on some pretext to talk, there are those nights when she neither answers her apartment phone nor her cell, and where his imagination sees her with another man. He tries to reject this proposition. He tells himself that if he avoided infidelity no matter the horrific consequences that ensued, then she would follow suit, as it was in both their natures.

He realizes she hasn't asked him about another woman in some time, and so contemplates asking her if she's met someone else, but he rejects the idea as too petty before it gains traction. He cannot avoid the doubts, however, as the issue of sex no longer seems to arise.

He often considers moving far away, to California or even another country, and just as quickly gives up the thought as unrealistic and irrational. At this point, the truth is unlikely to ever emerge. Even so he has researched and discovered that the penalty for concealing a body is more or less minor, but only if no larger crime is involved. He cannot, however, take the risk of such consideration if he confesses. Every time he contemplates admitting the facts of what happened that chilly May day he returns to his original conclusion that he simply may not be believed.

At times he wonders whether he should leave some written record of the events that led to her death. Something that could someday be shared with her family back in Austria and friends like the doctor, yet he knows such an action is absurd. Still it bothers him that no one else knows what has become of her and that she lies in an unmarked grave just steps from the Montauk Overlook parking lot.

He visited the site only once since he buried her and that was just recently. Only days before there was a hammering rainstorm steered by violent winds. The intensity falls short of a hurricane, yet the results are as unnerving. The deluge lasts through the night and into the next morning. Branches and even whole trees lie scattered across roads and lawns. Power lines are down. Areas closer to the beaches like Posner's actually suffer less from the violence as the storm flew in over land and not from the sea.

Posner waits a day, and then decides not to delay any longer. The town trucks come to clear the streets and the electric company restores power. It's time. The transient summer visitors are gone and those that stayed on to enjoy Indian summer have fled back to their permanent homes to avoid the worst of the storm. So it isn't a surprise that the highway from Amagansett to Montauk is relatively free of traffic at eight o'clock on a Thursday morning. Posner drives within the speed limit, yet is still riddled with anxiety as a police cruiser passes him going the other way. He has felt like this before and for the hundredth time wonders when the feeling will pass and concludes that it probably never will. Not as long as he remains a suspect, however distant and improbable that seems.

He pulls into the far side of the parking lot. The exact spot is etched into his memory and has been so for months. At first he's surprised at the absence of debris, and then realizes that the space has already been cleared of the storm's residue. Posner leaves the car and walks into the wooded area. He feels as if his body is simultaneously being pulled in two different directions. One part of him anxious to see that the grave is still covered, while another more desperate element is terrorized at the thought he'll find an exposed silver trash bag with decomposed limbs protruding from animal-induced tears in the plastic.

Away from the sun, a thick cover of trees welcomes him into a cool dampness. He walks tentatively down the slope. At first he isn't at all even sure he is in the right space, but some instinct takes hold, and then he sees the gnarled distended shape of the black pine and the roots he tripped over. The ground at the gravesite is still damp and covered with pine needles much like its surroundings. He can't tell whether anything has ever altered the soil. The undisturbed state of the immediate area after such an extensive storm is such that he doubts anything ever will.

He stands there and the memory of her presence sweeps over him. Almost five months and a few feet of topsoil separate him from any chance to reclaim sanity. He stands with one hand on the twisted trunk of the sand pine and loses track of time, although he couldn't have been there for more than a few minutes. The wail of a shore bird brings him back. He takes two steps up the incline when something catches his eye on the right side of the small clearing. Something small and man-made that doesn't fit lies half hidden under a curtain of pine needles. He moves to the spot, bends and pulls out the broken heel of a woman's shoe. It's sooty and gray but he can see it had once been white. It's Heidi's. No question. It's Heidi's.

Posner shudders. The heel must have somehow broken off when he tripped and dropped the body. Memory summons up the image of the tear in the bag and the white shoe sticking out. He can't imagine that in five months no one has stumbled on it. He slides the heel into the pocket of his windbreaker and trudges back up the hill, so oblivious to anything other than the cargo he carries that it isn't until he is nearly back at the Lexus that he sees a small blue car on the far side of the lot. A slight movement behind the windshield betrays the presence of a driver but the tinted window makes any recognition impossible.

As he drives away, he watches the blue car through the rearview mirror. A cloud of blue-gray tobacco smoke begins to float from the driver-side window until a surge of air tears it away. He's sure the occupant is watching him. It's nothing, Posner thinks. Just a coincidence. Someone just happens to arrive in the lot at the same time he comes out of the woods. The lot is empty except for his car, so it's natural to look at someone in an otherwise deserted place.

He keeps thinking about the man in the blue car. He assumes it's a man, as he accelerates down the highway then catches himself as he sees the speedometer race to over seventy. He eases off the gas, coasts into Montauk village, and stops at a drive-in. He buys a coffee, gets back in his car, and steels himself that he will not let such coincidences bother him. He sips half of the coffee and drives home feeling more in control. And to the extent he can exercise his will, he doesn't let the incident intrude on his life.

A few days later he stands in the middle of his living room and watches a procession of spindrift fly off rims of angry surf. There must have been a storm far out to sea, but the local forecast remains sunny with light breezes. For inexplicable reasons he keeps the heel, no matter the remote potential risk of its discovery. It rests in the zippered inside pocket of the windbreaker that hangs in the back of his garage together with other slightly out-of-fashion clothing he is not yet ready to give away. It is not by any means a trophy even though a prosecutor someday might call it such. No. He keeps it as a reminder of his own stupidity and the confusion between innocence and guilt.

The muted whirr of a phone call from Detective Wisdom draws him back. He hasn't heard from the police in several months. Wisdom explains that it's just a routine follow-up. Posner is happy Wisdom's not there. If he were he might hear Posner's sudden gasp as the detective announces himself, but whatever alarm he initially feels when he knows it's Wisdom, begins to dissipate in seconds.

"No. We haven't had any news on the disappearance, but we'd like to stop by and reconfirm a few matters. Whenever it's convenient is fine with us."

Posner regains his composure and suggests the following Tuesday at two. Wisdom confirms the time after consulting his calendar. Posner hangs up but is not as shaken by the surprise call as he might have been some months before. Maybe he really is getting more in control. The thought is comforting and he walks back and stands before the floor-to-ceiling glass that faces the ocean.

He loves the almost feral nature of the sea when it abandons all pretense of civility. He becomes engrossed in the abject wildness of the ocean and never once thinks to turn and look out the front window that faces the street. If he did, he would see a small blue car roll down his street and idle briefly at the foot of his driveway before picking up speed and moving away with its lone occupant, a man whose face he might remember, bent behind the wheel.

# CHAPTER 9

Wisdom's next day seems normal at first, and then gets more complex. He speaks to Brigid about the meeting he's scheduled with Posner and promises to try and reach Welbrook later that day. He leaves word with Bennett and the chief about the Posner meeting. In between other calls, he hears an old voice mail from Bennett, who relates the essentials of a message from a hospital administrator at Mt. Sinai.

> *Since you're the only one who's really still directly involved in this case, it's probably best for you to follow this up. Seems there's this rabbi of all people who wants to talk to us about Heidi. The name's Schmittman from the Maccabee Youth Center in Boro Park in Brook lyn. Seems Schmittman contacted Mt. Sinai Hospital who pointed in our direction. NYPD has more or less given up on this, so thanks for following it up.*

"What the hell is a rabbi in Brooklyn doing in this mess after almost five months," Wisdom wonders aloud, but there is no one near or interested enough to venture an answer.

He grabs his phone, leans his back just far enough, so that with his feet crossed on the metal desk, he and the chair are in a semibalanced state. He rocks slightly and calls the seven-one-eight area code number Bennett left. The phone picks up before the first ring ends and Maccabee Youth is announced by an energetic youthful female voice. He suddenly feels much older than thirty-eight.

"I'd like to speak to Rabbi Schmittman, please. You can say it's

Detective Peter Wisdom of the East Hampton Police Department concerning his inquiry about Heidi Kashani."

The voice says, "Wait a second," and Wisdom hears muffled sounds in the background. He tilts forward and manages to lift half a cup of tepid coffee with his left hand before his swaying motion begins to move him backward. He struggles to regain balance, but at the last instant some of the coffee splashes upwards until gravity draws it down onto his chinos where it produces a very predictable and raucous repetition of "shit."

"Is that any way to greet a lady?" asks a new voice.

"Sorry about that," Wisdom answers, but a part of him wants to laugh. "Just spilled some coffee. I'd like to speak with Rabbi Schmittman please."

"This is Rabbi Schmittman. And you're with the police. Right?"

Wisdom fumbles for a reply and resorts to a simple, "Sorry about that. Yes, I'm with the East Hampton police."

The answer seems to be enough.

"The reason I'm calling is that I just got back into New York last week after being away for six months and found out that Heidi hasn't been at the youth center in almost as long. When I called the hospital, they said she'd disappeared shortly after I left and referred me to a Sergeant Bennett of the East Hampton Police who said he'd ask you to follow-up."

There is a long pause before Wisdom speaks.

"It's true. She disappeared early in May on a day trip out here."

Thereafter it took only a minute for Wisdom to fill the rabbi in with an overview without mentioning any of the possible suspects.

"May I ask you how you know Heidi?" Wisdom has learned in such cases to always refer to the object of an investigation in the present tense, although he had already written off the chance of her still being alive. The rabbi's next comment shows she's struggling with the same issue.

"We were . . . we are friends. She's done a lot for the center."

"Like what?" Wisdom becomes more intrigued at the prospect of adding to the profile of the missing woman.

"She came to us about a year ago. I guess you know she's a resident in psychiatry at the hospital. One of our board members recommended her when we needed an experienced person to do some part-time pro bono counseling. She arrived a week later. Came direct from the hospital by a car service. Always wore a white hospital jacket and arrived every Tuesday at about five and stayed till eight. After a few weeks everyone began calling her 'The Woman in White,' like the title of the old English novel."

Wisdom just agrees. He'd studied English lit in college, but can't immediately remember details of that particular book, although something about the name resonates a familiarity. He's probably read it back when.

"So what exactly did she do at the Maccabee Youth Center?" Wisdom unknowingly pronounces Maccabee with the emphasis on the second syllable and the rabbi points this out after expelling a soft laugh.

"You pronounce it like an Israeli," she says. "It's the name of a popular beer in Israel although it's in honor of Judas Maccabee who led a revolt over two thousand years ago to throw the Greeks and Syrians out of Israel."

Wisdom doesn't know what to say in the presence of such knowledge, so he quietly moves on and asks again about what Heidi did at the center.

"Let me first tell you about what our mission is here. To make it as simple as possible we try to counsel those teens that have been through a serious family trauma. That takes in anything from child abuse, alcoholism, drug addiction, and the death of a parent, sibling or close friend."

"And this is only for Jewish kids?"

"No. It's open to anyone in the community, which helps us get government funding, but I'd say about sixty percent of the kids we treat are Jewish."

"Do you know why Heidi wanted to work there? I mean it's a pretty long trip once a week and she's not even Jewish."

"I know. On the first day she walked in she told us right from the start that she was Muslim, but that she wanted to work especially with Jewish kids. And everyone she counseled loved her. She was a very caring person. I can't believe she's disappeared just like that. There's this one young girl about fifteen. Her father was in the diamond business and was convicted of setting up a phony robbery to collect on insurance. It destroyed the whole family and this young girl went off on her own deep end. Started with drugs, moved out of her mother's apartment here in Boro Park, and drifted into prostitution. She was picked up for loitering and the precinct captain sent her over here rather than have her charged. She was here for less than a week with her mother's permission when Heidi arrived. Within a day she began to follow Heidi around like a puppy dog. She's back in school now and wants to study medicine like Heidi, but seems to be relapsing of late according to her mother. Without Heidi I'm not sure if she'll ever get back to what counts as normal. She idolized Heidi for her empathy, since she always made time for the kids, but also for her looks. Heidi's very attractive, but I guess you've seen pictures of her."

Her voice fades as she finishes. Then silence. Dead air. Wisdom grunts a "yes" into the mouthpiece to break into the stillness.

"Do you think she'll turn up?"

The weakness in her speech continues and sounds to Wisdom as if she's entered a period of resignation. Until then he'd almost forgotten he was talking to a rabbi and a woman no less.

"Honestly, we can't be too hopeful at this point. Too much time has gone by without anything to go on."

"I remember she had family in Europe. What do they think?"

"They have nothing to add," Wisdom notes, even as his mind wanders ahead and wonders how or even whether he'll approach Brigid and tell her about this side of Heidi. A side he was sure she'd never seen based on what she'd told him.

"Was Heidi particularly friendly with anyone at the center?"

"I'm afraid not, except for me, and even there we kept it very professional. I mean she never spoke about her social life, if that's what you mean."

"Did she meet any men there? I mean like relatives of the youngsters you treat."

"Not really. There were some other professionals around but nothing more than idle chitchat from what I could see and hear. Oh, once some doctor from Mt. Sinai met her here. I think his name was Henry something. I only saw him the one time, but he seemed as awestruck with her as some of the young kids, yet in an obviously romantic way. He seemed to get all steamed up when he was waiting for her in the lounge and she came out of the counseling wing talking to our resident senior social worker."

"What do you mean steamed up?"

"It wasn't anything he said, but I could see in his eyes. The jealousy, I mean. I think he might have smacked her right there if they were alone, but nothing happened. At least while they were here in the lobby."

Wisdom draws a breath and thanks her for her time. Then he remembers.

"It was Wilkie Collins."

"Excuse me?"

"The author of *The Woman in White* was an English writer named William Wilkie Collins. He also wrote *The Moonstone.* Some of the earliest mysteries ever written."

"I'm impressed," she said, the voice now much stronger than a few moments earlier. "I'm not used to policemen who read so extensively."

"And I'm not used to female rabbis," answered Wisdom.

"Well, I don't have a long beard, if that's what you're thinking."

Wisdom laughs, says he never imagined her with a beard, and then asks her how she managed to find such a profession.

"That part wasn't hard. My father is still a rabbi in Cleveland. And pretty modern. At first I had a hard time finding a pulpit, but then I came around to thinking that social work was more important. It's that simple."

Wisdom has nothing more to say although a part of him wants to stay on the phone and hear more about the Heidi no one else seems to have known. The few seconds of silence that follows tells him that there isn't anymore. He thanks her again, repeats his number in case she remembers anything else, and promises to call whenever they find out something.

It is only later, when he's home after changing into worn jeans and an old sweater, that the full impact of what she's told him sinks in. Seems that Heidi wasn't always the calculating predator of a person he thought she was. And it pisses him off even more that he'll likely never get to know the real person.

And then there's Henry who just keeps popping up like a garden weed. He also realizes he's thinking of Heidi in the past tense, notwithstanding what the rabbi said. "She's dead," he announces to an empty kitchen. "So let's see what our suspects think when she turns up at their doorstep. Especially Henry."

# CHAPTER 10

Henry Stern's life is falling apart, yet he seems to sleepwalk through the metamorphosis.

Memories of Heidi crowd out everything else that ever seemed to matter. His interest in medicine and in particular his residency in radiology evaporates. Three months after Heidi's disappearance, he is summoned to the office of the chief resident in radiology and given a warning to improve both his attendance and concentration levels. Despite this caution, he's unable to lessen the rate of his descent into melancholia. In one increasingly rare coherent moment, he confides to a colleague that if Heidi were there she would be able to treat his symptoms. But Heidi is not there and her absence is driving him over the edge.

He takes to sleeping in her apartment for which he still pays rent. He showers where she once did, and massages her shampoo into his hair until the recollection of her scent chokes him with memories of lust. He scrubs his teeth with her brush as he tries to suck the taste of her mouth back into his, but after the first month the essence of her presence has vanished as she did, leaving only a tasteless peppermint film on the stiffening bristles.

Her closet is barely filled as she has always disregarded the value of much clothing, but the pink-and-white dress that she wears for him on special occasions is missing. He knows she wore it on the day she disappeared from what the people on the bus reported. He knows how sensual she looks in that dress, and on more than one morning he lays half awake there in her bed and believes that she is in the other room wearing that particular dress, waiting for him to ask her to come back to bed. He begins to touch himself at first gently, then with more urgency and calls out to her. He actually calls out to her to join him, but as sleep slips further away, the reality of her absence seizes him more firmly, his partial erection vanishes and he can only sink a sobbing head into her pillow.

His performance at work further deteriorates and by the end of August he is put on an involuntary medical leave, but he is, in effect, suspended with the unlikely prospect of ever regaining his position. With nowhere to go, he wanders aimlessly through Manhattan streets. He takes up smoking again and begins to drink, but then just as suddenly stops the alcohol, preferring to ingest the Percocets he has accumulated from the hospital for his own use. There's also the Seroquel. He's taken it on and off for fifteen years after a shrink in New York said it would cure some of the hallucinations he used to have. There are times when he stops cold turkey, and then just as suddenly takes it up again. The day after he saw Heidi and some intern together he felt he was going completely nuts and started up again. Then a week later when he failed to satisfy her on that last night they spent together he knew it was due to the Seroquel. Now he's been off it for months, and he knows when he's off it he sees things no one else does. He also knows he's stayed off it because he's been hoping to find Heidi alive and anxious to get into bed with her again. But he feels he's losing control and needs to regain command of the search, so he decides to ease his way back on the meds. He can always stop later.

The dreams begin in earnest a few weeks after Labor Day. Slivers of such images have appeared and vanished over the past four months, but they are always so fleeting that he wakes with little recall except for the vaguest presence of Heidi. This is different. The dreams are full blown, exact in every detail and sound, and unlike any vision he's ever experienced.

The theme recurs. He is walking along an empty beach. To his right the ocean pants and growls as it pounds the sand. To his left the beach dissolves into clusters of scrub grass, which sporadically intersperses with jagged cliffs whose bases are partly eroded as if great chunks were bitten from a large cheese. The sun drops into the dunes behind him as he walks to the east. The air becomes cooler. The muted shriek of shore birds and the surf are the only sounds. Isolation welcomes him like a friend. He is almost at peace when he hears a plaintive cry. At first he doesn't recognize it, but then as the voice becomes stronger and more assertive, he knows it's Heidi's.

The voice comes from somewhere high and to his left. When he looks, all he sees at first is a gentle slope that rises from the beach. Beach grass and underbrush give way to sand pines and clusters of cedar. He strides up the slope with increasing urgency until it barely begins to level off amidst a thick stand of trees. He stops and listens for the sounds, which have become less frequent, then turns through a wide arc until he sees the shadow of a man carrying a body. The man is walking away from him so he cannot see the face, but the body he carries is clothed in pink and white. He knows it must be Heidi's. He bursts into a run, but actually falls behind the man no matter how hard he tries to keep up. He looks down and sees the sandy soil suck at his feet and pull him back as if he's mired in quicksand. In the end he's immobilized. He calls out to wait, but the man keeps walking until he disappears from view, and all Henry can do is drop to his knees and scream, a sound that always wakes him and is no longer part of the dream.

After the third night with the same tortured images, he concludes that Heidi was taken by one of the men out near the beach. He knows it's either Welbrook or Posner and this deduction makes the decision to stalk both men until he finds her whereabouts that much easier.

He arranges for a neighbor to pick up his mail, reserves a room at the motel in East Hampton he's used before, packs a bag, and rents a car at the neighborhood Avis. He feels better once he's on the road. As the city falls away behind him, he looks ahead at the still-crowded expressway, knowing that in less than two hours he will be that much closer to Heidi, and with the conviction that after everything's over, he'll be the one to save her from her abductor. His dream convinces him that she's still alive, hidden somewhere out there near the beach, and waiting for him to find her. And he will. He promises himself. That's all he has to do.

He arrives just as the sun sets and avoids the motel so he can drive to the nearest beach. He wants to breathe in the same air that she does before darkness encases him. He has no plans to visit with the police. He knows that he's still on their suspect list. They have made that plain in the past, harping on the coincidence of the car rental mileage, yet they have nothing more and have left him alone for several months now. He also knows, even if they may not be convinced, that he is innocent of any crime, save obsessive infatuation. He also knows that when he finds her he will dispatch the guilty party. In his minicooler in the backseat are two needles with enough insulin to inject his prey with convulsions, coma, and a certain heart attack. He will dispense justice if no one else will. He eats a quiet dinner at a small Italian restaurant in East Hampton and falls asleep early. His mind is clear and tomorrow he will begin to plan how best to stalk his quarries.

In some way it reminds him of hunting. He first went out with his father when he was a few days past his tenth birthday. He never knew his mother, who had died after a fall when he was barely three. So it was his father and a succession of housekeepers who raised him. The housekeepers who came and went like the seasons and who could never satisfy his father's standards in much the same way as he couldn't. There were many times when he wished he could also have been fired and sent away, but that was never to be. He had to succeed just as his father had succeeded. It was an early fall day just like today except that then he was in the Berkshires, and this is the beach. He remembered his first kill. He chased a white-tailed rabbit into a tree hollow.

"Don't waste time waitin' for him to get out," barked his father who had moved in behind him. "Shoot him right now."

And he did. It was easy until he pulled the bloody pulp out of the tree and threw up right there, his breakfast and bile spilling out and over the dead white tail.

"Now skin him, and when you're done with that, bring him back to the house, and we'll have the cook make us a stew for supper."

He did it all because he had to, but never hunted again and for all he knew maybe even became a doctor because of what had happened that day. But this was different. Whoever had taken Heidi had ruined his life and hers. The one who did it deserved to die, but a shotgun shell would be too quick. That's why he's brought the needles.

The needles each hold large doses of insulin. He had written the prescriptions himself. No problem there. He was still licensed as a doctor in New York state. More than once he pictures what will happen. He will force Posner or Welbrook to confess what happened to Heidi. Then he'll jab the man with the needle. No alcohol cloth to clean the skin. No bother to even roll up a sleeve. Just a simple large dose of insulin. So large the man's blood sugar will drop far below even common hypoglycemic conditions.

Posner or Welbrook will go into insulin shock. The skin will become cool and clammy. The skin color will pale. He might thrash about, but I'll be there to restrain him if he does. The speech will start to slur and convulsions will soon follow. Then a coma followed by a stoppage of breathing or heart failure. Just enough time to make him suffer without it being torture.

If there were emergency medical personnel around, they might recognize the symptoms and force-feed him pure sugar or orange juice, but that won't be an option. Everything will happen when we're alone. Just the two of us.

Stern decides to follow Welbrook the morning after he arrives. He drives to the modern house in Amagansett and is pleased to see the man's twenty-year-old shiny Mercedes parked in front. He lingers for a moment then drives on down to the end of the street and parks out of sight behind an empty construction dumpster. He turns off the engine and waits. After a moment he dials Welbrook's home number from his cell phone. Welbrook's voice picks up after two rings and Stern cuts off. The man is home. That's all Stern needs to know.

The front passenger seat holds a pair of binoculars, a brown package with a cheese sandwich, an apple, two bottles of water, and a package of cigarettes. The insulin needles rest in a small cooler on the floor of the backseat. He's prepared to wait, but after only an hour he sees Welbrook emerge wearing dark pants and a soft-looking tan jacket that looks like suede. The unique engine hum of a diesel signals Welbrook's on the move as his car rolls gently down the block in the other direction. Stern follows him at some distance. At this time of year he can see Welbrook's car with ease from thirty yards away.

Welbrook drives into East Hampton and parks near the Ralph Lauren store. The high season is over and Stern has no problem finding a parking spot some four spaces behind.

His eyes follow Welbrook into Ralph Lauren. From outside the front window he watches his quarry buy three shirts that are on sale at over one hundred dollars each and have them gift wrapped.

He trails the man into a few other stores, but these visits are brief.

After wandering for another fifteen minutes, Welbrook heads back to where he parked his car and enters the Starbuck's a few doors down. Stern watches him order a coffee, take a seat at a window table, and wait. Stern stands across the street in front of the movie theatre, leans against a parked car and periodically watches the image in the window sip from a cup. The wait isn't long. A man closer to Stern's age joins Welbrook, who stands to greet his guest.

The man has short cut dark hair and wears jeans with a sports jacket. They lean into each other as they meet and the convergence ends with a full kiss on the mouth right there in the nearly filled coffee shop. Welbrook hands the man the gift-wrapped package and they hug before sitting down.

The suddenness of it all momentarily paralyzes Stern. One of his two suspects has just openly announced he's gay and thereby removed himself from serious consideration in less than two minutes. And all of this happens after Stern has spent months agonizing over whether the admittedly attractive-looking Welbrook has ever fucked Heidi and is still hiding her away somewhere out here in some deserted dune cottage. He smokes a cigarette and then another before he reenters his car and heads to the motel where he can regroup and plan his move with Posner.

He decides to shadow Posner with more caution. Welbrook's unintentional revelation has increased the odds to infinite levels that Posner is the man he's after. He intends to follow Posner to the extent necessary to determine his behavior patterns and then confront him. Yes. He will challenge Posner to tell him where Heidi is hidden. And when he finds her, that's when he'll kill Posner. And then it'll just be Heidi and him. Just like before.

Posner seems less gregarious than Welbrook, as he seems to stick closer to home. Stern has chosen a spot for observation on the corner farthest from the house. His small blue rental car is barely visible from Posner's home, but not without some effort. Stern sits as he had with Welbrook, with enough food and water for a long day of waiting. This is what much of police work must entail, he thinks. Waiting and then waiting some more.

He positions himself that first day before seven and waits until the rain comes. It starts slowly, but after a few hours the wind gusts and sheets of water convince him that only a madman would attempt to move around and so he goes back to his motel.

He sits there in the small tidy room for nearly a full day while the storm hurls its engorged fury at the hamlet, which at that time is anything but a resort. At one point the lights go out, but the motel has its own generator and power is restored without incident. There is nothing Stern can do but wait and he falls asleep fully clothed. The night does not bring the expected dream, and he wakes not only refreshed, but convinced that he now closer to the truth and to the point where he can both rescue Heidi and exact justice.

When the weather returns to normal, daylight greets him with a cloudless blue sky. Even here, a mile from the beach, the storm's effects are obvious. Broken branches are strewn across the parking lot together with a miscellaneous assortment of rubbish, including broken lawn furniture, plastic garbage bags, and one red-soled flip-flop that lies perched atop a scattered pile of leaves. He walks to his car, brushes a small ragged branch off his windshield, and then walks to the office to see about the local roads. The news is not good. Trees and power lines are down everywhere. He is advised to stay close to the motel. In this regard he is lucky. A restaurant is open less than a hundred yards away so he won't be forced to drive anywhere.

He is reluctant to accept the fact that he will need to wait but refines his plans to catch up with Posner the next morning. Later that day he calls Posner's number to confirm his prey has not evacuated.

It is a possibility. He knows Posner and his wife have an apartment in the city but he guesses that Posner spends much of his time out here. To be closer to Heidi, he thinks.

Posner answers on the fourth ring, just as Stern is about to give up. So he's home. Good.

He hangs up without speaking.

He wakes early on Thursday and is so anxious to get to Posner's house that he forgets breakfast. He doesn't care, and is there just before eight. He parks down the block in the spot he'd chosen earlier in the week. It's another clear day. The streets here have already been emptied of debris and almost all of the houses are vacant. He rolls the window down and hears a still angry surf behind him as it says a final goodbye to the storm. Otherwise there is a stillness that unnerves him.

It is so calm that the sound of the engine starting on the blue Lexus in Posner's driveway shatters the air as if it were a thick and brittle object. He hasn't even noticed that Posner is already in the car when he arrives. He's lucky and knows it. Another few minutes and Posner might be off somewhere, and he would waste a full day's surveillance.

Posner backs slowly down the driveway onto an empty street. "He's a careful man. I'll have to remember that," Stern says to the empty passenger seat. He has begun to talk to himself aloud with some regularity in the past few months. Sometimes it's to Heidi, but more often to an unknown audience, a shapeless companion who agrees never to disagree.

Stern watches as Posner turns onto the main street and moments later accelerates onto the highway going east. He's easy to follow. There are few other cars in sight. But he must lay back more than a casual distance to avoid drawing even accidental attention. Posner stays at the limit of fifty-five although the road ahead is empty. A town police car comes from the other direction and Stern sees Posner's brake lights flicker as the cars near each other.

"What's he afraid of?" Stern asks aloud. "You're going slowly enough. Feel guilty about something, do ya?"

He follows Posner into the village of Montauk past the mostly empty motels and food shops. Posner drives through the village without stopping and picks up speed as he reenters the highway still going east.

"How much farther can he go? He's gonna be in the ocean pretty soon."

At this point there's no other traffic so Stern has to fall farther behind. He loses sight of Posner as the road bends and when it straightens out the blue Lexus is gone. Stern speeds up and goes for another mile before he realizes that Posner must have turned off. He makes a sharp U-turn and speeds back the other way. He barely looks at the road ahead as he scans both sides of the highway until he comes to a sign announcing the Montauk Overlook turnoff and wonders why he didn't see it when he first passed. He slows and enters the parking lot and sees the blue Lexus on the far end where it's hidden from the main road.

He pulls into a spot as far from where Posner parked as he can and still keep it in sight. There is no movement in the Lexus. Now he must decide whether to exit his car or wait till Posner returns. He squirms with indecision for a few minutes, then decides he just can't wait and opts for leaving his car and moving with as little sound as possible along the fringe of the woods until he approaches Posner's car. In less than a minute he's close enough so that a subtle noise draws his attention down the slope. Posner is stooped over the ground and picking up an object. From a distance Stern can't identify the item but he sees Posner put it into his windbreaker pocket and look around furtively. For an instant Stern thinks he's been seen, but

Posner's subsequent stride up the slope without a second look convinces him otherwise. He races back to his car, considers taking off, but then decides he'd rather Posner be unnerved about being seen.

He lights a cigarette and watches as Posner exits the woods and looks in his general direction for a moment before he reenters the Lexus. Now he's been seen. He's sure of it. He watches Posner hesitate then put his car in motion. Stern slides down the seat and half turns the other way to avoid any possible detection.

As soon as the Lexus clears the parking lot, Stern pulls ahead to the area where Posner parked. He gets out and moves down the slope. He's heading for the gnarled sand pine that he noticed moments before. He reaches the area in seconds, but there is nothing special to see. He scans the ground. Maybe there's more of what Posner picked up, he thinks, but he sees nothing but pine needles and cones. He turns in an arc one last time. He'll have to come back again. There is no need to remember the spot. The gnarled pine is a good landmark, but he remains puzzled as to why Posner would come all the way out here for just a few minutes. Back at the parking lot, he uses a felt-tipped pen to darken the base of the sand pine closest to the edge of the lot, so he'll know where to park the next time.

He drives back westward through Montauk and passes the Lexus parked in front of a drive-in restaurant. "Surprised he's not stopping at a bar for a real drink," he says to his unspecified companion before he dissolves into a spasm of giggles.

That night the dream returns, but there's a difference. He wakes moments before the end, just as the shadow carrying the body disappears from his view behind some trees. He doesn't scream. Every sensation in his body tells him she's dead and that the shadow carrying her body is Posner's. The landscape in the dream is familiar. He's been there. That very day he walked among the same sand pines in his dream. The thought drives him awake and all he can think of now is an image of Posner burying Heidi's body. He has to prove it to himself. He doesn't care anymore about the police. They've been useless. Even imagining him as somehow involved is idiotic. No. He'll have to find some evidence and then confront Posner. He relishes the thought of seeing Posner sweat and plead for his life, knowing that it's a plea he will not grant.

The next day he goes to the hardware store and buys a shovel and a flashlight.

"Looking for night crawlers, are ya?" asks the woman behind the counter.

"Something like that," Stern answers as he wonders over the woman's unintentional insight.

Then he drives to Posner's house. He sees the car in the driveway, pulls up, and calls the number, but it's busy.

"Too bad. I almost wanted to reintroduce myself," he says and exhales a stream of mock laughter. Then he turns the car to the east and begins to drive out to the Montauk Overlook.

After a few minutes on the highway his voice returns to normal. "There must be something in that area near the gnarled sand pine that he wants to hide. He must have been the one carrying Heidi. What do you think?"

His companion's silence affirms the assertion.

Everything about the drive to the overlook seems mechanical. He drives at maximum speed along the highway, slows through Montauk village and accelerates again until the overlook turnoff. The spot he's marked on the base of a tree the previous day is still there, but he realizes he could have found it easily enough without the marking. One car is parked in the lot near where he pulls up. Actually, it is a small white pickup with the words "Marine Patrol" printed on the side and rear. He presumes it's some official car and prepares himself to wait until the occupant moves. He turns on the radio and lights a cigarette. The wait isn't long, as a uniformed officer of some kind appears from the far side of the lot. The man raises a small hand in greeting.

Stern nods and raises a hand in reply. He tries to act like he's a local by remembering how the men he knew growing up in a small town in the Berkshire foothills would greet each other and strangers alike. Friendly, but not too much so. It seems to work. The man smiles back, enters his truck, and drives off.

Stern waits ten minutes to see if the man plans to return. A heavy cloud cover sits over the area and a chill seeps through his sweater. He feels he should have worn something warmer, but the first few steps down the slope convince him that he will soon have enough exercise to heat his limbs. In seconds he is back at the gnarled bent pine. He randomly starts to dig. The sandy soil is soft from recent rains and the ground carves with ease under the shovel's blade. He digs a wide swath around the tree creating a perimeter encompassing the area he remembers where Posner walked. None of the trenches are more than a foot deep. He works for fifteen minutes, stops, and then begins a new search area at a spot some ten feet farther down toward the shore.

After nearly an hour all he can show for his effort is sweat. He begins to fill in the trenches, but doesn't take the time to smooth out the soil, or brush pine needles back across the surface. In his haste he fails to notice a two-inch square of silver plastic torn from some bag that became mixed in with the soil.

# CHAPTER 11

Peter Wisdom looks across the backyard lawn of his sister-in-law's house, smiles, and raises a half-empty can of Bud in the direction of his wife, Karen. She smiles back. Karen stands out among the other women plucking bits of sliced vegetables or chips from the platters on the picnic table. She is short, but her smile is never ending.

He stands near his brother-in-law, Rollo, who tends to the steaks and burgers on two adjacent grills. It's a family Sunday afternoon picnic. Rollo lets his staff set up the restaurant today, but he'll go over later when it starts to get busy. Wisdom's son, Kevin, kicks a soccer ball around with his two cousins and a neighbor. It is a sweet, early fall afternoon with far more sun than chill. He wonders if sweet is the right word, but decides it'll do.

His family's been in East Hampton long enough to be considered locals. It started with a summer vacation cottage his father bought in the area called the Springs when he got out of the army and began working as a New York City firefighter. That's when they lived in Queens. Wisdom was the youngest of two boys and one girl. He remembers that they spent most summers at the cottage, and then year-round weekends after his father expanded and insulated the house. His sister still lived in Queens as did his brother who became a city cop as soon as he was old enough to take the test.

Peter Wisdom was going to be different. He went to Hofstra and studied English lit and marketing, but when it came to working at it after graduation, his interest in business cooled. That's when his father suggested he take the Suffolk County Police exam and move into the East Hampton house where his parents were by then living full time when they weren't spending the winters in Florida.

He took the exam, passed everything, and did particularly well on the physical part; the sit-ups, pull-ups, and mile-and-a-half run. He didn't need to wait too long after that until East Hampton town asked County for a list of those with local addresses who passed the exam. He was near the top of the list and began within a few months. Nearly fifteen years later he was one of the more experienced detectives on Bennett's squad. He married a local girl who teaches English at the East Hampton Middle School and they bought their own starter house in Sag Harbor. Not a bad way to live, he tells himself with thanks every morning. Not bad at all.

He puts down his beer and leans against the wall at the back of the patio. It's a nice crowd, not too big, maybe twenty people or so. Friends and relatives. They try to get together a few times every year either before or just after the high season. People talk about family, their jobs, or the aggravation of summer visitors, but they rarely ask him about his work. He understands. People he's close to know enough not to ask him to remember stuff he'd rather not talk about most of the time.

He looks again at Karen. She's in animated discussion with one of Rollo's neighbors.

She's very beautiful and for the millionth time he wonders why she picked him. She could have had any guy. And if he's so lucky, then he wonders why he was so attracted to Brigid. Or even weirder why he was attracted to the picture of Heidi when he knew she was very probably dead.

He tries not to think what he might have done if Brigid had really come on to him instead of just playing a role. He tries not to think of the guilt he might have created, and even now, knowing that she was playing a game to prove a point, he feels guilty for even having these thoughts. And he hadn't even done anything. He shakes his head imperceptibly and reaches for the beer. He takes a sip then puts it back down. Too warm.

He leans back against the building and looks up at the top of trees on the edge of the property. He muses that while sex may be a very strong drive, the actual act can never take too long. But guilt can last forever. He shudders. With him it would. Happy he's never been unfaithful or even close.

Oh, there was the time shortly after their marriage when he answered a call about a possible prowler. He hadn't been on the force very long and was working the eleven to seven Montauk shift one night when a late call came in about a prowler.

"Better get over there just to be sure," said his dispatcher's voice, with a film of lilt atop his normal crankiness.

It was a small cottage at the top of Tuthill Road up past the lobster store, but in January everything was flat-out quiet. Even the sound of his cruiser seemed to splinter the night. She answered the unlocked door, a fortyish woman with long straight black hair and an oversized nose on an otherwise average face. The only unordinary thing about her was a barely closed bathrobe.

"The noise came from in there," she said, and pointed to a room behind her.

He moved ahead and found himself in a small bedroom. He moved to the window and checked that it was locked. It was.

"No problem here."

When he turned she had one foot up and resting on the still-made bed, but her robe had become a bit undone. He had a clear view of her upper thigh and a dark patch beyond. Above her waist he had an even better glimpse of one rather large breast and an erect pink nipple. He took a deep breath, moved back through the front door, and didn't turn around till he was halfway down the porch steps.

"Best keep that door locked," was all he said, barely looking at her.

Even before he got into the cruiser, he felt his heart hammering away and the sweat on the back of his shirt. He reported in that everything was quiet. When dispatch answered, "You've done a real quick check," amid background laughter. He knew he'd been had. Seems they set up all the rookies with this one nympho. But he laughed about it with them later and there'd never been anything close since then. And that was twelve years ago.

He'd been innocent then and he's innocent now, but a seed of guilt still runs through his brain about the way his body reacted back there at Brigid's house. He knows it's stupid and if he told Karen, she'd probably laugh at him, but he still decides it's better not to tell her. What's the point? Someone once told him about a *Playboy* magazine article years ago where Jimmy Carter admitted that he'd lusted after other women in his heart, but never did anything. If a born-again guy like Carter can own up, then why is he so bothered? He wants the whole issue to go away. Maybe it will by next week when he has Brigid meet everyone involved. Then she'll go back to Europe and the idea will crawl away. He remembers something else. No one's gotten back to him about setting up a meeting with the good doctor Stern. He pulls a notepad from his pocket and jots down a reminder to call Bennett, who's acting as liaison with NYPD.

He moves to the large tub of cold drink cans floating in icy water and chooses a Diet Coke. Just then Karen appears with two paper plates overflowing with steak, corn, and salad.

She gestures to one of the tables where he sees Kevin already busy biting into a burger between yapping with his cousins about whatever. A nice normal American weekend afternoon, he thinks and smiles at the simplicity of it all. In this little setting, they're a million miles away from a missing, likely murdered, woman. It never ceases to amaze him how his work and its emphasis on the unexpected negative aspect of human nature runs so close and yet so far from ordinary behavior. Today's optician could turn out to be tomorrow's axe murderer. At least that's the kind of issue they talked about at length in the criminal psychology course he'd once taken.

"You were deep in thought over there. Anything you want to share?" asks Karen.

"Just that I love you," he says, meaning every word.

The next day he gets a call from Bennett.

"They can't find Dr. Stern."

Bennett's voice seems hoarse, almost fragile. Wisdom hopes he hasn't started smoking again.

"What's that supposed to mean? Did they try the hospital?"

"That's something else. Seems he's been suspended. His performance had dropped off the charts in the past few months, and they must have felt he'd become a risk to patients. They certainly weren't looking for a bunch of lawsuits down the road. Anyway, he hasn't been in the hospital for well over a month."

"Friends? Colleagues at the hospital? Family?"

"Nothing there either. He was a classic loner. Some of the other residents didn't even know he was gone, but maybe they work such crazy hours that it's not the kind of thing you notice right away."

"Think someone scared him off?"

"Don't see how unless the sister got in touch with him and told him to beat it."

"That's not possible. She doesn't even know who he is."

"You sure about that?"

"Hell, Brigid hated Heidi's guts."

"I asked if you were sure."

Wisdom pauses a second before he affirms.

"Okay then. We'll have to start looking and assume it's just coincidence. When were you going to spring the fake Heidi?"

"This week, I hope. I've already lined up a meeting with Posner. Welbrook's just about off the radar screen for now, so after Stern he's the only one left, but all my money's still on Stern."

"That's what I thought. Any chance of postponing until we're sure everyone's lined up?"

"Guess so. Don't think Brigid's going back for another two or three weeks."

"Then let her know we might have to delay. In the meantime we'll try to see if we can check into his background a bit more. He used to live upstate. That's where he said he went on the day she disappeared. Remember. That's when the mileage clocked the same as to East Hampton."

# CHAPTER 12

Dr. Henry Stern isn't lost, in hiding, or even trying to run away. He is at that moment sitting and watching Posner's house from the same spot he's used before. He uses a worn but serviceable pair of binoculars. He follows Posner as the man moves about on the second floor of his house. Posner seems nervous and anxious. Good. He will keep up whatever he's doing as the man is losing it. At this thought Stern begins to laugh. At first it sounds more like a cackle in a barnyard, but later it comes out more like someone out-of-control, almost alien.

After he finds out the full truth about Heidi, he plans to kill Posner. He's never taken a life before, although there are those who might believe otherwise. He was seventeen and an all-around everything in school. Sports were easy. Ditto school. The only problem he ever had was with girls. He was afraid to ask anyone out and even more fearful he'd be rejected. It all came together during the summer before his senior year. He'd been trying to work up the courage to ask out Rosalie Sanchez for months after she transferred in, but never had the guts to try. Then on a late August night a few weeks before school would restart he saw her at the drive-in, whose parking lot was where everyone in the town under the age of twenty joined up on warm summer nights.

She was hanging with some guys he didn't know very well and holding a paper bag with a beer can she greedily sipped at. She was pretty and dark and very well built. He worked up enough nerve and offered to buy her a soda or a hot dog. At first she looked at him with level serious eyes, then just laughed and told him the only hot dog she wanted was the one between his legs. Before he could react she moved right up to him till they were eye to eye, zipped him open, and fished out his cock. He was anything but ready and she took hold of his stumpy limp dick in a soft hand with bright red polish on her nails and held it for barely a second before she dropped it.

"Too small," she said. "Think I'll throw it back."

And with that everyone laughed. Not just she, but also the guys she was with, and then everyone else who either saw or heard what had happened. There were also many who were happy to laugh at him, either for the pure humor in it, or in many cases for the opportunity to take down the big little man on campus; the students he'd outscored on exams, and the athletes he'd bested in team tryouts were all there reveling in his tormented humiliation.

He stood and watched her slide alone into a used and much dented canary-yellow Chevy convertible with a broken muffler and a tailpipe that was tied to the undercarriage with wire, yet still managed to graze the ground with a shower of sparks when the car moved. He watched her drive away to the baffled thumps of hot air raging through the torn metal gaps beneath the car while she saluted him with a crimson-tipped middle finger while all he could do was shout.

"You bitch. I'll kill you for this. You hear me? I'll kill you."

And then she was gone, and he fled moments afterward, oblivious to the night or the road, ostensively going home, but actually wandering to try and rid the foul reek of shame. He lost track of time until he moved across the Beaver Flats Bridge and saw the rear end of a yellow car tilted in a twenty degree angle to the nearly dry creek bed it had fallen into. He stopped the car and saw the tire marks where the Chevy couldn't hold the approach curve and tore through the modest wooden railing before dropping forty feet into three feet of mud and water.

That's where the police found him. It seemed like moments, but he later reckoned it had to be more than fifteen minutes. He told the police that he'd left his car off the road just before the entrance to the bridge and gone down and around to the creek bottom where the Chevy had hit and stuck at a strange angle. It was quiet except for the small splashes frogs make in chorus with the occasional night bird. He looked in the driver-side window and at first only saw one arm stretched out with the fingers turned upward. He didn't try to look at her face, but he still remembers the red nails reaching upward in some kind of plea. He raced to the nearest phone to call for help, then returned to the bridge to wait.

The cause of death was a broken neck, but an autopsy showed she was legally drunk. At first there was all manner of speculation. The most prevalent idea was that the two of them had met up by accident and he killed her, and then tried to cover it all up by running her car off the road with her already dead. There was, of course, not a shred of proof for this theory, and the fact that he was the one who called in the accident and was still at the scene when the police found him worked more to his innocence. The final inquest reported an accidental death. There were still, however, many in the small community that believed then and probably still believe that he killed her. And now he was a suspect again, but he'd show them. He'd show them it was Posner.

He never returned to his local high school and his father's business and political connections enabled him to pull in some favors on short notice to get his son into Deerfield Academy that fall. That was the time just before he began having hallucinations about Rosalie Sanchez. He had promised to kill her and she died. Simple as that, but it wasn't going away. His father brought him to see a series of mental health professionals where he was diagnosed with a very incipient form of schizophrenia and put on a series of antipsychotic medications. There were side effects, of course, but over a period of time, the worst of these, the dry mouth, blurred vision, and drowsiness ebbed to the point of minor factors he could live with.

Then it was Yale premed and Downstate Medical in the city. He never lived in Hillsdale again and sold the house after his father died. He was smart and capable and his paths through college and medical school were relatively easy. At the time he met Heidi, he was in one of those intervals when he wasn't taking Seroquel. He knew he could always self-prescribe when the bad feelings returned, which made him feel like he was sharing his body with another person. No one at the hospital knew of his condition. Such records were confidential and would remain that way unless he alone decided to unseal them.

Several months into their relationship, he began to feel those symptoms again and he went back on his meds. And that's when he began to experience sexual failure. Some call it erectile dysfunction, but it was all the same to Heidi. Viagra didn't help. He knew she wouldn't keep him as her lover if he couldn't fuck her as often as she wanted. After just a few such incidents he stopped his medications. That was his only hope. He was prepared to live with whatever twists and turns his mind would take as long as he had Heidi. But Posner took her away.

Yes. He wants to kill Posner. For several years his work involved saving lives, but this is different. All those people back upstate who might still think him guilty of murder would get their chance to be right. He was innocent then, but now he was prepared to confess his guilt as soon as he finished the job. He catches a movement at Posner's front door and puts the glasses down. His prey is on the move again.

"Oh Lordy, Lordy, this is so fucking good," he says to the empty seat and starts the engine.

As soon as he sees Posner's car head east on the highway, he knows the man's going back to the Montauk Overlook.

"She must be buried there. She must. I just missed the spot, that's all. Now he'll take me there. He will. I know it."

Then he smiles and begins to hum as if to remind himself that he's just out for a drive in the country.

Amos Posner's on his way back to the overlook. He can't help himself. He suspects that someone's been watching him and wants to see that the grave is still undisturbed. He's had the feeling for a few days now. Ever since he got the call from that cop Wisdom. It started with the small blue car in the Overlook parking lot. Just sitting there. Not doing anything. Just watching him. At first he thinks it must be the police, and then decides it's just coincidence. But he's seen that same blue car a few times in the last week. Once he even thought he saw it parked on the far corner down the block. Now he assumes once again it's the police. Who else could it be? His hands are sweating as he grabs the wheel tighter than necessary.

He can't let his nervousness show. He's just passing through Montauk village when the full reality of it all hits him. Maybe the police are trying to spook him. Trying to make him commit some act of self-betrayal. Maybe it really was Wisdom. That's when he sees the blue car. Maybe half a block behind. As he approaches the far end of town, he starts to slow then jerks a quick left across two traffic lanes into a service station. He pulls up alongside a pump that blocks most of his view of the road. Still he has a fleeting glimpse of a small blue car speeding the other way as he pulls to a complete stop, but there's no time for a clear look at the driver. Even after he turns the engine off, his fingers tighten around the wheel, as if he were trying to squeeze the life out of it.

Henry Stern sees Posner veer off, yet can do nothing. He goes a bit farther down the road and turns left toward the harbor. He thought he was careful, yet not enough, otherwise why would Posner have pulled over? He turns his car around and pulls onto a grassy area where he can watch the eastbound traffic in case Posner changes his mind. He waits for over an hour before he gives up and returns to his motel. Maybe it wasn't such a good idea to follow Posner too closely. Maybe now that Posner recognizes his blue compact, the idea of frightening him into a mistake has become self-defeating.

He checks out of the motel after looking up the addresses of a few guesthouses in the area from the phone book. He notes the address of a local Chevrolet car dealership.

"A switch to a Chevy would be fitting. Don't you think?" he says to his unseen companion. "A kind of tribute to the late Rosalie Sanchez who'd fuck anyone but me. And look where it got her."

He pays his bill in cash. He has paid all his expenses in cash so far, except for the rented car. He drives to the Chevy dealership and surveys the lot. After a bit, he wanders in and asks about a short-term rental. One or two weeks should do it. "Just to give it a good test drive. Yes, I know it'll be an expensive rental for two weeks."

He thanks the salesman, says he'll think it over, and then drives back to Posner's neighborhood, but he's already decided not to do anything with the dealer. Too much information to give up. He doesn't know how he'll handle things from now on, yet he isn't worried.

Henry Stern has come to believe in premonitions. He also appreciates that certain events have fallen into his lap; like the time he happened to show up just as Posner was leaving to drive to the Montauk Overlook. He feels such happenings are preordained and that Posner will at some point lead him to Heidi's grave. He has already acknowledged to himself that she is gone and that Posner has killed her. Now he must watch the man like a hawk and wait for the mistake. This is why he again sits in his car a block away from Posner's house.

It's not the most comfortable place to wait, but he has nowhere else to go. He plans to sleep in his car and at about eleven that night he sees the lights go off in Posner's house. He waits another fifteen minutes then gets out of his car to stretch. He walks aimlessly up the nearby driveway of an oversized modern house. He is about to turn back when he sees the garage door lock set vertically, in what is usually the open position. He tries it and it opens. He carefully rolls up the door and looks inside. The light from the gibbous moon is more than enough to illuminate a parked car. A white Chevy Malibu no less. A Chevy. Another omen. Not just a coincidence. He tries the connecting door between the garage and house and finds it open. He calls out without response. And then again. Still silence.

Inside the house is all whitewashed walls and bleached wooden floors. He passes through the kitchen and into a living room with empty leather armchairs and sofas.

"Abandoned for the season, are we?" The lack of vocal response confirms the obvious.

"Well not for long."

The portents are too numerous. His mind works in overdrive and in less than ten minutes his blue Ford rental rests in the large garage alongside the Chevy while he stands at the window of an upstairs bedroom with a clear unfettered view of Posner's house. He sets his watch alarm for six and falls asleep. That night he doesn't dream.

# CHAPTER 13

Peter Wisdom is about to call Posner to delay their meeting when he finds himself on the receiving end of Posner's call. At first he thinks Posner might also want a delay, but that's not the reason for the call. He seems agitated and raises a different issue.

"I am pretty sure someone's following me. If it's the police I want you to know your department's way out of line to try something like that."

Wisdom barely waits for Posner to finish before he denies it all.

"There is no one from our department following you. Believe me or check with Chief Ferris. There is no interest in following you. All we wanted to do was go over some of your earlier comments about the missing woman. In fact, I was just going to call you to reschedule."

The last part is, of course, completely true and the denial of interest completely false. He's used the same line before with potential suspects when he didn't want to give them a heads-up.

"What makes you think someone's following you?"

Posner hesitates, and then clears his throat. Just like that, Wisdom's put him on the defensive.

"There's this blue car. It's been following me around for the last few days. I couldn't see the driver, but I know it's been following me."

"When was the last time you saw it?"

"Yesterday morning."

"Where was this?"

Posner hesitates. Maybe he shouldn't be bringing this up at all. He's about to say he isn't sure, but he knows that sounds too evasive.

"It was on Montauk Highway. I was taking a short drive toward Montauk."

"Where to?"

"Why is that important?"

"In case someone was following you for a reason. Like they expected you to lead them somewhere."

"Oh. I didn't think of that."

But of course that is exactly what Posner had thought about when he called Wisdom. And now things were getting messed up. Too much so. He holds the phone away and bites into the air to slow himself down.

"You still there?" asks Wisdom, who wonders why Posner seems to be pulling back.

"Yes. Sorry. I was clearing my throat. Let's see. I really wasn't going anywhere special. Just out for a drive. I do that a lot."

"So where did you first notice the car?"

"I think I saw it in my rearview mirror on the highway. Then when I got into the village and it came closer, I could see it was the same small blue car I'd seen hanging around my house the day before. I stopped and let it go past and I was sure of it."

"Recognize the driver?"

"No. It went by too fast and I had just stopped."

"Okay," Wisdom sighs into the receiver and sips from a small bottle of Poland Springs.

"What can you tell me about the car? New? Size? Make? Whatever you remember."

"It was small and blue. I think domestic. Kind of shiny so I guess it was new."

"Anything else?"

"Sorry. That's all I remember."

Wisdom draws another breath.

"We'll look into it. You can be sure. And if you see a police cruiser in your area, it'll be one of ours just looking around for your friend. Now as long as you're on the phone, I did want to postpone our meeting. Something came up on our side."

"Till when?"

"Just for a few days. Let's shoot for Friday. At about two. I'll confirm in the morning. Is that okay?"

"It's okay," says Posner, but in the back of his mind, he still sees things building up too fast.

Events are closing in on him. Then he remembers that Sara will be out on Friday, and he won't be alone, but Wisdom has already hung up.

Wisdom can't hang up the phone fast enough before he calls Bennett, but all he can do is leave a message. He paces, squirms, and chews at a fingernail for twenty minutes until Bennett calls back. Another two minutes to update Bennett. Afterward there is only silence.

"You still there?"

"Yeah. Just looking for something that came in yesterday from NYPD."

"What's that?"

"Seems our doctor friend rented another car from Avis. We tracked him through his credit card. Guess what kind of car he took off in?"

"Don't know the model, but I bet the color was blue."

"Bingo! And for the record it was a new Ford Focus. Supposed to get good gas mileage. By the way, in about five minutes you should get a color photo of the car courtesy of the Ford PR department."

"So the doctor is out here somewhere. This could turn into a big problem since he's already told us he thinks that either Welbrook or Posner are involved in Heidi's disappearance. Guess Posner was right.

I mean, he *is* being tailed. Now we just need to find the doctor. The way this is going, any linkup with Brigid could be a real donnybrook."

"Then it'll have to wait a bit till we find the good doctor. Time to put out an APB on Stern's car. It's quieter now so patrol can pay more attention."

"I'm on it. I'll fill the chief in then check all the places where he might be holed up. We've got a pretty complete listing of places he could stay and things are relatively slow, so I can put a few people on it. If he's here it shouldn't take more than a few hours. That's unless he's staying at some friend's house."

"I doubt that. From what I remember, he doesn't know anyone out here."

"Except for Welbrook and Posner."

"I've already arranged to have a car cruise regularly by Posner's house. Welbrook lives in the same neighborhood, so we can double dip the surveillance."

"Good. So what do you make of all this?'

Wisdom hesitates in silence for almost ten seconds before he speaks.

"Four things.

"One. I think the doctor killed Heidi. I know it's still only a hunch, but he did have the motive of jealousy, as well as the opportunity when he disappeared for a day in a rented car without an alibi.

"Two. I think she's probably buried out here somewhere unless he found a way to lose her in the ocean.

"Three. I think he's been trying to pin the deed on either Posner or Welbrook."

"What's the fourth?"

"I think he's nuts. I mean the doctor."

They agree on two points. One is that it's still too early to officially bring in County although Bennett will keep them warm. They also plan to speak again as soon as Wisdom hears back on the possible location where the doctor may be staying. He collects the car photo and arranges to have all cruisers in town have a copy together with the doctor's description. His orders are to identify, report in, and follow the subject without being noticed, but not to approach.

Wisdom's done all he can think of. He wants to update Brigid, but decides to wait until he knows more. He's prepared to stay at his desk all night. As it turns out, he gets a message about Stern within thirty minutes and calls Bennett without even dropping the receiver.

"He was at the East Hampton Motor Inn. At least until yesterday morning. Stayed there about a week. Paid in cash but gave them a credit card as security when he first checked in. Also used his real name so he wasn't looking to hide his identity or anything."

"Anyone know where he went?"

"Negative."

"So he could still be around town somewhere."

"That's for sure, only he might also have taken off when he figured that Posner made him. I mean he might have left our little piece of paradise and decided to either come back later or drop the whole thing."

"What whole thing?"

"That he wants some kind of confrontation with either Welbrook or Posner. Who the hell knows what that could lead to?"

"And we've got to watch them both because Stern probably doesn't know Welbrook's no longer a probable."

"Roger that. And I'd better fill in Welbrook just to be on the safe side. I'll also see if I can scare up a few unmarkeds to watch both houses."

"Good. How's the sister, Brigid?"

"Okay, I guess. I'll have to call her later. She deserves to be filled in, especially with a possible mental case roaming around."

Later turns out to mean about four thirty. He's done everything else he could think of. Now they need to wait and see if Stern turns up, either around here or back in the city. He checks in with NYPD, but Stern hasn't returned to his apartment and Avis says the car is still out.

That's when he decides to call Brigid, and only then does he realize why he'd been putting it off. He's embarrassed. They've spoken only once to set up the first appointment with a man Wisdom referred to only as a "local," but he hasn't seen her since that afternoon at her house. They both knew that her brief dress-up time had turned him on. He doesn't want to feel that way again so he hasn't called. It's a stupid sequence, so he breaks the cycle and calls. The phone rings four times before the machine clicks in. It's funny. He hears her voice, but at the same time it doesn't sound like her. He leaves a detailed message and hangs up. He's actually relieved he doesn't need to talk with her at that moment. In a way he's broken the ice without the need to go farther.

By six o'clock nothing turns up and he decides to head home. During the drive, he tries to evaluate whether Stern might now be physically dangerous. He still thinks the doctor is putting on a big act to shift blame to another, but he can't discount that the man has likely already killed. His assumption is that if Stern feels cornered, he might well become violent, especially in a confrontation with Welbrook or Posner.

He manages to shower and change into jeans and a sweatshirt before dinner. Karen's made a root vegetable stew with some of her food co-op's autumn overflow.

"I assume that you're giving some of this away because even if you use the stuff up at this rate there'll be enough left for the whole winter," he says as he manages to fish bits of parsnip, potato, and carrot onto his fork.

The phone rings before she can answer, but he knows she'll distribute most of it to a local food pantry. Karen answers and in a moment puts her hand over the mouthpiece.

"For you. A woman. Sounds foreign."

He takes the receiver and slips a few feet into the hallway. He's aware that his fingers are wet and he wipes them on his jeans.

"It's me," Brigid says and somehow makes it sound like a secret lover calling.

Wisdom instantly regrets having given his home number out, yet he's done it before.

"What's up?"

"After your message about a delay, I thought some more about the idea and—"

"And what?"

"And I think that maybe I was wrong. That I don't want to do it. Any of it. I mean I don't know if I can do it. Whether I can be her."

"But you're not her. From what you've told me you could never be her. The idea was to try and catch a guilty person and it was your own idea."

"I know. I know. Do you remember the day when you came over here? When I tried on the dress so I could look like her."

"I remember."

And just like that his memory serves up an image of the way Heidi looked that afternoon and his reaction. No. Not Heidi, it's Brigid, asshole. But what's the difference? Really? Brigid or Heidi. The effect was the same. Heidi's picture and then Brigid in the same dress.

"Are you still there?"

"I'm here."

Got to regain my balance. Take control.

"What happened to make you change your mind?"

"I guess it's the idea itself. And then your message said there would be a delay. I kept thinking about what I was going to do. The more I thought, the more I felt I didn't want to be her. Not even for a second. When I made myself up like she does and wore that dress I couldn't change back fast enough. Do you remember what I told you?"

"Yes. That you felt dirty."

"Yes. I felt dirty."

Neither spoke for several seconds. Wisdom heard her breathing return to what must pass as normal.

"Was that your wife on the phone?"

"Yes."

"She sounds very nice."

"She is."

"Are there children?"

"We have a son. His name's Kevin. He's eight."

"Well, I won't keep you from your family any more. I just wanted to tell you that I'd prefer not to go ahead. But if you still feel it's important, I will. Is it still important?"

"I think so, but it's still up to you."

"Then let me know what you decide. I did promise you I'd do it and I will. It's funny. When I called you tonight, I was planning to tell you I absolutely didn't want to go ahead. But now that I've told you why, it isn't so important anymore. Thank you for listening. Call me when you decide what to do. Goodbye."

Wisdom doesn't have a chance to speak before he hears a dial tone. He didn't have time to tell her that now there's a risk in going ahead with her plan that they hadn't given much thought to up till now. Even if they decide to go ahead, he'd have to fill her in on the possible danger, however remote. He moves back into the kitchen and Karen looks up.

"Sorry about that. She's a possible witness in the disappearance case."

"Is that the sister you told me about?"

"Yes."

"What's she like?"

"She's from Europe."

"I mean what's she like, I could tell she was foreign?"

"Nothing special. A woman trying to forget about a problem she had with her sister a long time ago."

"Will she?"

"Will she what?"

"Forget about her problem."

"Time heals lots of things. For her, I think it will take longer than most."

# CHAPTER 14

Posner sits alone on the top step and looks down at the red quarry tiles that in seconds changed his whole life. A part of him still thinks he's been caught up in some colossal hallucination. Heidi is, in fact, just a fictional character. Someone he's never met and only dreamt about. A make-believe person conjured up from a movie or book who died right here. Although they've been bleached and then washed many times, he can never look at the tiles and see anything other than splattered blood.

He moves down the steps and stands at the base of the stairway. The hall light is on directly above his head, as it has been on constantly since that day. Some part of his brain insists that every step be visible so no one can ever fall again. He bends down and draws his fingers across the cool tiles, eventually moving them into the gray channels of grouting. Some of the grout now has a lighter shade where he's applied some bleach. His eyes bore into the floor with almost radiographic intensity, but his sight cannot penetrate the tiles' façade. There is no trace of blood, yet he knows that chemical tests would prove otherwise. An objective observer such as a real estate appraiser would describe the space as the entrance area of a modern house in a beach community. The red tiles are not exceptional. There are tiles like these in probably half a million homes across the country, but these particular tiles are matchless. They alone and uniquely have been an instrument of death.

He leaves the house in faint darkness and enters his car. He looks around, but there in the early dawn sees no sign of the little blue car. Maybe he's still sleeping, he muses as he releases the hand brake and rolls down the driveway. He also doesn't see the police car that Wisdom promised. Probably too early for them as well. He looks at his watch just as the hands form a straight line from twelve and six.

The highway ahead is empty and spotted with wisps of ground fog. He keeps checking his rear mirror, but there is no sign of another car. In the east, the sun rises to meet his eyes above the horizon of wooded hills and lofty dunes. At this hour it's an oversized orange ball that summons him even as it jumps from dune to dune atop the highway as he moves eastward. There is warmth in this light that is almost spiritual. It signals him with a beacon's energy to return to the overlook and check to see if the man in the blue car or anyone else has been there.

His conversation with Wisdom convinces him the police have not been involved. In retrospect it was a smart move, however uncomfortable, to draw them in, if only to further defray any possible suspicion. Although he has not seen the face of the man in the blue car, he is sure it must be the doctor boyfriend, Henry. Posner has no reason to suspect this other than by deduction. Since he was one of the few people on the bus who spoke to Heidi, the doctor has probably targeted him and whoever else was there as suspects. Yet the doctor hasn't a shred of evidence to link Heidi to him or else he would have already given it to the police. His trip this morning is to insure that the spot near the overlook still remains in its natural state after his first encounter with the blue car.

He arrives at the overlook just as the daylight begins to march across the pines. He has no need of a flashlight although one lies in his trunk cradled by a rake and shovel. They have rested there in the same place without use since that evening in May. Everything has long since been cleaned; the trunk vacuumed of obvious sand traces and the shovel's shiny steel blade washed and dried.

The air at this dawn hour delivers a sharp chill that slices through the fleece sweatshirt under his windbreaker. He disappears into the pines at the edge of the lot and is swallowed from view if there was an observer, but he's alone. He's already checked and waited several minutes before leaving his car and setting out into the trees.

He soon comes upon the space and lurches to a wobbly stop as dawn bathes the area near the landmark pine tree in a pale orange. He immediately sees the ground's been disturbed. Someone's been here in the last few days. He bellows a string of curses as he moves around a few random shallow remnants of holes that radiate from where he knows the grave site lies. He approaches the unfilled areas and starts to scrape soil with the edge of his shoe into the remaining open cavities. In minutes he is done and steps back against the gnarled sand pine to observe his effort. His breath comes in short bursts from the effort, but he feels satisfied until he realizes that the area still doesn't look untouched. Twigs, pines cones, and needles aren't as random as they should be. The space definitely looks as if there have been recent visitors. A new chill dances across the back of his neck. Not from early morning dampness, but from the renewed fear of discovery.

He tells himself to stay calm and think. The grave is still undisturbed, so whoever was here failed to find anything.

"Good, good," he repeats aloud as he jogs back up the hill to the lot, fixated on what he must do next. The sun is higher now, and the lot is already half-washed in light. He pulls the rake from his trunk and returns to smooth over the soil. The work is so easy he nearly laughs until he remembers that a body rests just below his feet. He pushes the pinecones and needles back into some reasonable random pattern. He stops and inverts the rake to pull some clods of wet soil from its tines when his fingers grasp the utterly foreign texture of silver plastic, just like the material in the bag he used to bury Heidi.

Posner stares at the tiny silver flake between his fingers, an indestructible polymer that will survive all normal conditions save fire. He looks again at the ground. Maybe there's more he thinks, but he soon verifies that his fingers hold the sole confirmation that anything was ever put in this sandy soil. He puts the artifact in his jacket pocket and realizes that it now rests alongside the bit of broken heel. One last look at the site verifies that he has returned it to a semblance of its original state. He walks back to his car. It is nearly seven and the lot is still thankfully empty.

He drives back toward home, yet he doesn't want to be confined indoors just yet. He pulls into a beach access less than a mile from his house and looks out over a calm ocean. Again he's alone. It is as if all the people have gone. Except that he knows they haven't. Wisdom is there and the man in the blue car whom he might as well start calling the doctor. He's the one who worries Posner far more. Anyone who stalks someone like that could be dangerous. Wisdom didn't mention any possible danger. Maybe he didn't want him to worry, but now he's worried all the same. What if the doctor comes looking for him with a weapon?

Think! Think! He's got to sort this out.

He opens the door and leaves it ajar as he walks a few steps onto the beach. It's the same beach that he took Heidi to so many months ago. He pictures her standing there only a few feet away, posing in a pink-and-white dress with the spray of the surf soaring in the background. A vivid image of her posing him for a photo morphs into one of her sitting on his couch, legs spread around a black patch, and then immediately transforms in a flash of color as he imagines her falling in a grotesque cartwheel down the stairs creating a pool of blood. He shudders and gasps until his pulse calms.

He's almost back at his car when the simplicity of a strategy hits him. There is no reason to believe that the doctor will ever cease his harassment. If he is obsessed with Posner, the stalking can only continue and lead to confrontation. In such conflict only one can win. And to Posner this only means that only one can live.

He drives back to his house in a sudden state of relaxation. As he leaves the car at the top of the driveway, he is engrossed in thought and fails to look around. If he had turned a full circle and had far better eyesight, he might have even seen Dr. Stern peering out from the second floor window of the house down the street and at the far opposite corner. But he neither stops nor turns. His mind is engrossed entirely on the upstairs bedroom closet shelf. Somewhere in the back of that shelf beneath a carton of old sweaters there is a small box. It is a relic from Sara's brief tenure some years before as a State Supreme Court Justice, compliments of her extensive earlier activities on behalf of the Queens County Democratic Party. In the box lies a revolver. Posner hasn't seen it in years and it may not even work, but he does remember that Sara has mentioned cleaning it at least once a year, so it should be okay.

He finds it almost immediately and pulls the box down and rests it on the bed beside him.

It's not locked, yet it still takes time to bring himself to the point where he slides the lid open. When he does, he sees the weapon, a Smith & Wesson Chiefs Special that sits on the cushion of a soft hand towel. He remembers that the revolver is compact, which makes it lighter than many handguns. He also recalls that it only carries five rounds. Beyond that he can't remember much from the one lesson he had years before on loading and firing. He knows it would be a comforting thought to have the gun available if the doctor invades his home, and so he lifts it from the box. He stands and holds the revolver as he had been taught in his right hand with the left hand steadying the right wrist. He pans the room. There is an unmistakable sense of power. At first he thinks he would be afraid to use it, but just holding it allows him to feel like a different person. The only issue now is whether he waits for the doctor to come to him or he seeks him out. He thinks that it would be better to meet him on his own terms, which means here in his home where he could easily claim self-defense against an intruder. As his mind runs through this scenario, he realizes that just the act of holding the gun permits him to no longer fear this man and he decides he is prepared to kill if necessary. No. More than that. If he is to ever have peace again, he will have to kill this man. He replaces the revolver in its case, slides the box closed, and returns it to a lower shelf in a spot that's easier to reach.

He walks to the door, then stops, turns, and faces the floor-to-ceiling bedroom windows. The shades are open and a concentrated beam of white outside light slashes across the room. "An artist's light," people have called it; an indigenous element that runs throughout the East End of Long Island that supposedly attracts creativity in the fine arts. Such enlightenment is not on Posner's mind at that moment. His eyes follow the shaft of light that arrives and settles on the king-sized bed. He cannot help but imagine for the thousandth time what might have happened if he'd taken her hand and moved into the bedroom instead of allowing her to slip into eternity.

They have sex, but he is far from perfect. Too far. It's all over in minutes. They dress without speaking in what seems like seconds and the silence continues as he drives her back to the bus stop. She walks from his car without a goodbye and he goes home. End of story.

That is how it might have been. Maybe he would have felt guilty, but that could have passed by now. She might have mocked him, but he would have deserved it and nothing more would have ever developed. No one would have died. His earlier fears about federal crimes would return as his only worry.

✦ ✦ ✦

He calls Sara to find out her travel plans. This will be her first trip out since that day. She says she's getting a lift and is already in the car with a neighbor's family who are coming out for a few days. They've left early and traffic is light. She won't be too long. She's anxious to see him.

Everything's changed in the last month. Things between them were still in limbo, trapped somewhere between reconciliation and the edge of collapse, until he arrived unannounced at the apartment one afternoon. He knew he was losing her. Or driving her away. It was all the same. She might even be seeing someone else. He's thought of that and worried about the possibility. And the jealousy of it all made him want her like he hadn't in months. So he'd made a decision to surprise her and see where things went. Maybe she wasn't interested anymore, but he had to find out. When he opened the door, he was half afraid someone else would be there, but she was alone. Even so, her only greeting was a glare. When she spoke her voice was clipped and impersonal.

"What are you doing here? I thought you were back at the house staring at the ocean. And how long has it been since you were here? A month? Longer?"

She moves to the living room window, turns her back to him, and appears to stare across the street at the corner of Third Avenue and Ninetieth. He stays in the middle of the room, several feet from the door he's just entered. One hand leans against the polished wood arm of his favorite wing chair. A small bag rests at his feet. He takes a step toward her and then stops. He almost wants to ask her if she's missed him, but decides it's wiser not to go there.

"It's only been a few weeks plus a couple of days since I was here."

"It seems longer."

"I can't help what it seems like."

"You can't help anything anymore."

She turns back from the glass and faces him. Her eyes widen. He feels the heat of anger.

"For months now you've been distant. You've changed. You can't keep sweating out what the Feds might do, or keep cursing the bastards at your old firm for throwing you to the wolves. We've covered all of that already, and I'm fed up with your self-pity. All you've done for several months now is sit around the beach house and keep away from me. It all started back in May. Did something happen then? Something that made you change even more?"

He ignores the fact that she's the one who's been distant and wanted to separate, yet realizes that she isn't accusing him of having an affair. Not this time. His reaction spills out. Almost too fast, but he has prerehearsed a possible answer for months.

"No. I swear. It's nothing. And it's not you. I just can't take the city anymore on top of my issues with the Feds."

"Bullshit! You've worked here all your life."

"It's not the same when you're not working. Now all I sense is the crush of people, the noises, the trash, and, most of all, the loneliness of someone without a place to go."

"This marriage hasn't had a place to go either. It's close to being finished as far as I'm concerned."

"Stop it. I love you."

That's when he should tell her about what happened. But he can't. He can swear fidelity all he wants, but fidelity was what got him here.

"Then prove it."

Her voice has softened and is now throaty and barely audible. She again turns back to the window without waiting for an answer, but he knows that if he says or does nothing it would all be over. Done. Finished.

He doesn't speak again, but moves up from behind and presses into her. The window reflects a faint yet true image of her eyes closing even as her mouth parts to pull in short breaths. She moves a few inches, as if to reaffirm the source of the pressure. They stand like that. A car horn blares from the street, but they don't move. Not an inch.

"Get undressed," he says at last.

There's no answer, but she doesn't move away.

"Take off your clothes before I tear them off."

The smile in the reflection widens.

"Go ahead and tear away, but take care of the blouse. It's silk."

That's when it all changed. She wants him again and that's all that matters. He still isn't sure why, but his sex drive is all the way back and it elates him despite all the issues that still exist. He still hasn't told her about what happened. He can't. He knows she senses his worry and assumes she just attributes it all to his potential matters with the Justice Department. Now it's much too late to tell her the truth, although he longs to do it.

He sees a light out there somewhere. He can't risk losing her after he came so close. The longer he's waited the less likelihood there is for anyone to believe him. All he can think of now is deflecting attention to Stern if it comes to that. Our marriage or Stern? No choice. No choice at all.

Her attitude has also made a complete shift in the past month. It's clear that she now seems to want to put the past behind them and make a new start. In the past few weeks she often speaks about moving away. This is new. She says she's grown tired of the firm, the hours, and the useless feeling she gets from some of her clients. She says more than once that she's mostly tired of not being with him. Since he'll only stay in the apartment for limited periods, her solution is to switch her career and move if he wouldn't mind.

Wouldn't mind? The thought makes him positively giddy, and he embraces the idea. Yes, sell the apartment. Yes, sell the house. He can bear it he says as he withholds his hope that he might never again see the red quarry tile floor. She even has a future career plan. A law school friend is a dean at Cal-Davis in California. There's an associate professorship opening in corporate reorganization law available and she's interested. What does he think? He doesn't hesitate to affirm her idea. A new start for both of them. And it's all her idea. Wonderful. Now all that's left is to take care of the doctor.

He goes back and reenters the bedroom. He pulls the box from the closet and moves it to a shelf in the upstairs hall closet just feet off the living room. What better place to keep a weapon than near where he would entertain an unwelcome visitor. He moves back into the main room with the ocean view. He's ready in case the doctor decides to pay a visit, although he has doubts the man would actually try.

# CHAPTER 15

She leans into the cushioned backseat. Her eyes flutter closed.

"Relax. Grab some sleep if you like." Ed Whelan's voice is soothing. He's even been told he sounds like warm syrup.

"It's just past noon and we're between rush hours, so we should be there in less than three hours."

Ed and Frances sit in the front of the Volvo and listen to Beethoven's Pastoral Symphony on a CD. The volume is down. They have an apartment a few blocks away from the Posners' in Manhattan and a house just around the corner in Amagansett, which makes it easy to give Sara a lift to or from the city when the timing works out.

The music rolls through the car in quiet waves. There's an image of a forest clearing. Red-and-yellow foliage enclose the open space. A spotted fawn stands nearby and arches its neck toward a low-hanging green morsel. After several minutes, Ed tilts his head toward the backseat and blinks his eyes a few times. Frances nods.

"Yes. She's asleep. Let's be quiet." She mouths all of this.

There's no need for speech. They've already played catch-up gossip an hour earlier while they waited in their car for Sara to come downstairs.

Frances keeps pivoting her head to view the front door of Sara's apartment house while they speak. It wouldn't seem right to have Sara interrupt them.

"She was really shaky when we met for a drink several months ago. First his old firm screwed him over for doing what they asked him to do. Then they hung him out to dry when the Feds got involved. He seemed to be handling it pretty well though until last spring. That's when she said he fell into some kind of deep depression and shut everyone out. Especially her. I gather they might even have separated for a while. I know she hasn't been out to the beach for months."

"Is that when she thinks he started an affair?"

"She never said that. I've already told you, I just picked up some vibrations. It's my hunch. But maybe I misread the signs. Maybe I was wrong."

"Honey, you're not usually wrong about these things. And what makes her so pure? Remember a few months ago I told you that I thought I saw her walking arm in arm with some guy out of a steak house on Forty-Seventh Street."

"That means nothing. It was probably business."

"Even so."

"Even so nothing. Whatever either of them might have given into is gone now."

"What makes you think that?"

"Simple. When she called and asked if we were going out this weekend and wanted a lift her whole attitude was different. She was anxious to see him. Even ventured that he'd changed. And all for the better, so I assume whatever it was he had going on was over. She also said they might be moving out West sometime soon. Said she might get a teaching job at a law school in California. I asked her if we could have first dibs on their apartment if they sell. She laughed at that. You don't laugh at the idea of selling your apartment unless you're either happily getting divorced or staying married. And I don't think they're getting divorced. Not after speaking to her."

"I hope so. Amos is good people. They both are."

✦ ✦ ✦

Frances glances at the backseat just as Sara opens her eyes.

"We're only about an hour and a half away if the traffic holds."

Sara nods and smiles just as her cell phone rings.

"It's Amos," she says as she looks at the caller number unable to suppress a widening grin.

# CHAPTER 16

Stern wakes just after six and curses after he sees that Posner's car is gone. He resigns himself to wait. What else can he do? He wanders through the house he's appropriated and searches the kitchen. He finds a plastic bag with frozen bread in the freezer along with a quarter pound of butter. The only thing in the refrigerator is a large bottle of Evian. He unscrews the cap and drinks a third of the bottle. He checks the taps and confirms the water is still on and so he uses the bathroom. His face in the mirror is somehow unfamiliar. The deep shadows under his eyes confirm his recent stress.

While he slept, thoughts spun through his mind about how to confront Posner and whether to somehow engage the police to be there. He knows that if they're present he'll have to give up any idea of harming Posner, at least at that time. He still wants to either follow the man or drag him back to the overlook area to the spot where Heidi is buried. And he's sure of it. Sure that Heidi lies near where he saw Posner. That's why he's so mad at himself for not being awake when Posner left. He can't search the whole area without Posner to show him exactly where. At that moment, almost in mid-thought, he decides right there that his best plan of action is to just knock on Posner's door and take it from there. He finds a tube of toothpaste in the medicine cabinet and works a dollop of Colgate across his teeth with a finger. He needs a shave but doesn't bother. He doesn't need to be clean shaven to confront a murderer.

He moves back to the bedroom window with his binoculars and

waits for Posner to return. He picks up his cell phone and turns it on for only the third time since he left the city. There are two messages. The first is from Detective Wisdom from the East Hampton Police Department. They'd like to meet with him as soon as possible to review some aspects of the case. They'd tried his New York apartment, but he wasn't in, and would he please call them at his earliest convenience?

The second is from the neighbor he'd asked to get his mail. A policeman had stopped by to see if he knew where Stern was. That was all. He checks his home phone next. There's just the one message from Wisdom that repeats the sense of the one on his cell phone. He looks up just in time to see Posner pull his car up the driveway. He watches as the man moves into his house with an almost carefree abandon.

"Have you decided something, my friend? Well, I have. I'll see you soon. No doubt about it." Stern laughs as he speaks, and the words tumble from his mouth with a hysterical edge.

He moves back to the kitchen and drinks more water. He checks the case holding the lethal needles. The only issue that remains is whether to contact Wisdom. For now, no one knows where he is. That's good, he thinks. Fuck the police.

# CHAPTER 17

Wisdom arrives at his desk later than normal, courtesy of his annual departmental physical. Except for a slightly elevated blood pressure reading, which will be rechecked in a month, everything else looks fine. A particular report he's been awaiting sits in his in-box buried under assorted other matters. It takes him almost an hour to get to it.

The report is a GPS summary of Stern's recent cell phone activity. There was a call to Welbrook's home from a site quite near Welbrook's home. Then two days ago he'd called Posner's home from somewhere in town. And this morning there were two calls: one to Stern's apartment and one to his cell phone voice mail. Both calls were made from a location only a few hundred feet from Posner's home. He asks the department's resident techie to check out and see if the calls were made from the street or a house. The GPS chip in Stern's phone is a new one, unlike Heidi's. This allows them to pinpoint the source of the call to within a few feet.

He checks in with the patrol cars doing drive-by surveillance on Posner's home. No blue car was seen in the vicinity on any drive-by over the past day. He asks patrol to go back again over an area within a few hundred feet of Posner's house while he waits for a more exact answer. He tells them to look for any sign of human activity. Do the houses look occupied? Any lights on? Are there cars in the driveway? Anyone walking in the street?

Looking at the report, it has occurred to Wisdom that Stern may have left the blue car somewhere else and could be hiding in the area.

How else could he explain the location of the source of the calls and the absence of the blue car? He decides he will need to advise Posner to stay indoors until he visits him.

He calls, but Posner's line is busy. Then he dials Brigid's number. She answers after three rings.

"It's Detective Wisdom here."

"Hello, Detective. How can I help you? Are we on for tomorrow?"

"Not sure yet about tomorrow, although I frankly doubt it. But there is something I have to tell you. I should have mentioned it already, but I first thought it better not to be too specific."

"Please go on."

Brigid is being quite formal, and the tone makes Wisdom all the more comfortable.

"There are two possible suspects who might be involved in Heidi's disappearance. One's a local from out here. The other is a doctor with whom she had a relationship when they worked at the same hospital. The doctor hasn't been home for a few days, and we have reason to believe he's stalking the guy who lives out here."

"Because the man who lives out here is responsible?"

"Maybe. But we think it's more likely that the doctor is the one involved because of jealousy and that he's trying to shift suspicion to the guy out here."

"So what do you want to do?"

Wisdom smiles at her pronunciation of what and want, with a vee instead of a wah sound.

"First, I wanted to advise you that if these two men meet up, there could be some danger. We already know that the local guy's been followed and we also know that the doctor's been traced to near where the local guy lives. In short, I don't think we should go ahead with the plan, at least for now."

"But if not now, then when? I really do need to go back to Geneva in the next few weeks."

"I know, but I won't risk the possibility of putting you in any danger. It's neither smart nor department policy."

"So that's it? The whole idea to try and trap one of these people is over. Just like that. After all the planning and your meetings with your superiors."

She pauses for a breath, but Wisdom is silent.

"You're telling me it's all over. I'll go back home and never know what happened."

"That's not true. We'll continue to look into this. Fact is, I'm planning to stop by the local guy's house sometime later today. Maybe the doctor might even show up. Anyway, I'll stay on this disappearance till we find out what happened to her. Believe me."

"I do believe you, Detective; I'm just not satisfied with your decision."

Wisdom hears the connection go dead, but if it hadn't, and he understood her faintly mumbled mixture of Farsi and German, he would have heard Brigid speak aloud to herself about what she planned to do next without his help.

# CHAPTER 18

The decision makes her a bit nervous, yet she continues to plan details without hesitation. She will wear "the dress." That's what she's come to call it, "the dress." She pulls it from the closet and checks the seams and length. She's only worn it that one time when Wisdom came to the house. She did feel dirty as she told him, but she also felt that it gave her a different look and ultimately a power she'd never experienced before.

She lays the dress out on the bed together with a bra designed to enhance her cleavage. She knows the effect it had on Wisdom and assumes it will be the same with the others. She's already showered and washed her hair. There is nothing more to do now except dress, but first she kisses her ears with a daub of Heidi's favorite Lanvin perfume. In minutes she's ready.

Her rented car, an Audi A-4, sits in the driveway. She hasn't used it much, trips to the supermarket and post office, one dinner meeting with Vice Consul Weis and a whirlwind tour of four art galleries on a rainy Saturday afternoon. She would have liked to have spent more time with Peter Wisdom. More social time, but she knows he's married, and apparently happily so, and she is not like Heidi. Definitely not like Heidi. Most of her days are spent sitting right there with a view of the ocean and a book in her lap. She knows it's time to go back to her life in Geneva. There is nothing more here for her other than pain, and so it's time to end it all.

She moves to the small desk near the front door and lifts a large manila envelope. Inside sits a folded map of the area with two circled addresses. There is also a sheet of paper with three names complete with addresses and phone numbers. The names are Stern, Welbrook, and Posner. She ignores Stern's Manhattan address and concentrates on the other two. She smiles as she remembers Wisdom's attempt to camouflage the identities by speaking of "the doctor" or the "local guy." She's had all the details for over a month courtesy of Herr Weis of the consulate. All he needed to do was call in a State Department favor, but that's what his job is 50 percent of the time, isn't it?

She stares at the three names in front of her. Why did Wisdom only speak of the doctor and one other man? The man Wisdom called a "local." The doctor was Stern. That was clear. The other two men, Welbrook and Posner, live close to each other according to the map and addresses. One of them must have been discarded as a suspect, but which? And why?

The why isn't really important. All she needs is the name of the local man, either Welbrook or Posner. She can't approach both and leafs through a small book of local numbers she keeps until she finds Bennett's number and takes a chance. The connection is quick.

"Can you help me? I'm supposed to meet Detective Wisdom, but I'm not sure if it's at Welbrook or Posner's house."

"That's odd," says Bennett, knowing the disguise plan might have been delayed, but thinking that they would arrive together if it was still on.

He quickly answers, "At Posner's. Do you have the address?"

"Yes. Thank you. It's very close."

One last look in the mirror and she's ready. In minutes she's driving down the highway and senses the freedom of knowing she'll soon have the truth. The earlier tension she felt has evaporated. She's prepared to risk that Bennett might call Wisdom and relate their conversation. Still, this is not a worry. She's not frightened. This is all too important. The road ahead is vacant, so she pushes the Audi to seventy. She flies along past clustered sentinels of black sand pines. It is as if the car knows the same urgency. "*Gut,*" she murmurs. In minutes she'll be there.

# CHAPTER 19

Stern decides to drive the Chevrolet he finds in the garage instead of the rented Ford. It's only to the corner, but a car should be available if he needs to make a quick exit. On top of that, he feels that there may be a need to remain less obvious since he assumes a description of his rented car is known by now. He slips on his jacket, comforted by the slight pressure from the nodular shape of the two toxic syringes that press against his torso. He has no more with him. The rest were back in the apartment in the city. So be it. These will have to do.

A final look through the window confirms that Posner's car still rests at the top of his driveway. This last look is fortunate. Just as he is about to leave, he sees a police cruiser swing around the corner and stop just in front of the house where he's hiding. He ducks his head away out of instinct. There is no way the police can see him from where their car sits.

He expects the car to pull away, but is surprised when a patrolman steps from the car and approaches the front door. He hears a bell ring. And then again. After ten seconds there's a knock on the door, which precedes the rattle of the front door handle. Then the bell again. He moves farther away from the window, yet the bell seems to follow him. Then silence. He moves back to the window and looks out. The car is there, but no policeman. He waits and barely breathes. After another few minutes, he hears the static from the man's radio before he sees him. The cop is talking on his handheld.

"The house seems empty and all doors are locked." Stern then hears a “Ten-four,” before he watches the man return to his cruiser and drive down the street where it slows as it passes Posner’s house then moves on until it disappears around the corner.

He moves downstairs to the garage connecting door and abruptly stops with his hand on the door handle. How could they possibly know to look here? Then it’s clear. They somehow can trace his cell phone. He enters the garage and slips behind the wheel of the Chevy. The keys are on the dash where he first saw them. The remote door opener is clipped to the visor. He presses the button and watches the large double door swing open. The car starts immediately and he rolls it down the short driveway into the street where he makes a quick turn down the block. He sees Posner’s house looming above him, a kind of Holy Grail he’s about to grasp.

The word about the absence of any activity in the house temporarily occupied by Stern reaches Wisdom just before he’s about to try Posner again. This time he’s more successful and wastes no time as he gets directly to the point.

“We have reason to believe that Dr. Stern has been in your neighborhood, at least earlier today. Have you seen anyone hanging around your house in the past few hours?’

“No. Nothing.”

“What about unusual street noises or phone calls?”

“Nothing there either.”

“Okay. I do want you to know that we have reason to believe Dr. Stern might be dangerous.”

“Thanks, but I’m sure I’ll be fine.” As he speaks Posner stands and looks down the corridor towards the hall closet. “Yes. I’m sure I’ll be fine.”

“Well, just so you know, we’re having a cruiser pass through your neighborhood at regular intervals.”

"That's very thoughtful. Oh, Detective. A question. Do you think this Doctor Stern was involved in the woman's disappearance?"

"It's a possibility, sir. There are many possibilities."

"I see. Okay. Thanks again. Bye."

Posner feels almost giddy when he hangs up. He no longer fears discovery. The doctor is now the one between the crosshairs and has probably always been the one. No. He is no longer afraid. Sara will be here soon and they can start planning for a new life. He strides to the credenza and opens a bottle of wine. As he pours a glass he remembers that this was the same vintage that he opened for Heidi. He hoists the glass to toast her memory, and then watches as if petrified while his hand begins to shake and a flow of red trickles over the edge and onto his fingers. It's Heidi's blood. That's all he can see. He splashes the wine out of the glass and across the sink. He washes his hands, but still sees her blood. Whatever elation he felt moments before was just a single, almost fragile speck of time that vanished. All he can think of now is wanting Sara to be here with him.

He sits until the images of blood begin to fade and thinks of Sara. He knows that the car that carries her is the new black Volvo of their New York friends and Amagansett neighbors. Door-to-door service is a nice luxury for anyone who heads to the Hamptons on a weekend. Even now, after the high season has past, there are still many part-time resident owners who have become more devoted to their weekend escapes. And the numbers have grown of those who now spend more time in the area especially after 9/11. He remembers the rush of New Yorkers who took out safety deposit boxes in droves after the attack. He still continues to puzzle at the possible contradiction in logic when he considers why they still live in the city most of the time but keep their birth certificates in East Hampton.

He also remembers the unease he felt whenever he went into the city after 9/11. He kept thinking that another attack could happen again, maybe on a subway, a bridge, or tunnel. A few months after the attack, he asked Sara if she would consider moving full time to Amagansett.

"They have lawyers out here too," he'd said, but she put him off.

"But mostly for real estate and DWIs," she'd answered. "And I do neither."

Spoken like a merger-and-acquisition specialist, he later thought, but to this day he still feels some relief, however small, when he leaves New York. Not exactly like abandoning paranoia, more like cleansing away a bad taste, but he also knows most others no longer feel the same, if they ever did.

That's another reason why he's so excited to see Sara and go over their plans. Things are getting closer to normal and that's good. Very good. And for him maybe there'll be only one more trip to the city. Two at the most. He settles back into the sofa. He begins to feel a warm goodness wash over him like the mist that rolls across the beach when the ocean is still cool and damp warm air flows in from the southwest. He smiles and stands. Now he's ready for that glass of wine.

Stern parks in the street at the bottom of the short driveway. He checks his coat pockets for the tenth time in the past five minutes to reassure himself the syringes are still there, and then strides up the driveway and mounts the three steps to the door. For some reason he checks his watch. Two fourteen.

"It's time," he says aloud. "I'm coming, Heidi. I'm coming."

Then he raps on the door.

Bennett reaches Wisdom on his cell phone.

"I thought you'd like to know. I just had this odd call from your Austrian friend Brigid."

"What about?"

"She said you were supposed to meet and wanted to confirm it was at Posner's house."

"Did you?"

"About ten minutes ago."

"Dammit! She's trying to do it all herself after I told her we were scrubbing the operation because it's too dangerous. So now she goes off on her own. I'll get my ass right over there. Stern's also been lurking around the neighborhood. Can't risk getting her caught up in the middle of anything. Bye."

Wisdom runs down the corridor and through the front door while he calls dispatch and asks them to have a cruiser get to Posner's house and meet him. And no one is to be allowed in or out till he gets there. No one.

Posner hears the knock. At first he thinks it's Wisdom or that Sara's misplaced her key.

He moves down the steps and opens the door to a smiling Stern. It's already too late to go back up the stairs to open the closet and reach for the gun. Stern walks past him without speaking, climbs the stairs and turns.

"Where did you bury her?"

No introductions. Certainly no handshakes or small talk. The words come out in a sharp staccato. Posner follows him up the stairs and moves to the edge of the hallway near the closet before he turns. One eye on Stern, one on the hallway as if to reassure himself that the closet hasn't disappeared in the last few minutes. His fingers begin to shake and he slides one hand into his pants pocket to mask the tremor.

"I don't know who you're talking about."

"You know damn well. Heidi. Heidi Kashani. The woman you picked up on the bus. The woman you fucked and then killed. That's who, you shit."

"You're confusing me with someone else. Calm down. If you're talking about that unfortunate woman who disappeared on the bus several months ago, the police have been here and we've talked, even more than once, but there was no contact after she left the bus."

Posner had already developed this strategy of absolute denial as an initial tactic, but he can see it isn't working after Stern speaks again.

"You're lying." Stern's voice rises. He's almost screaming. He pulls a large syringe from his inner coat pocket and approaches to within three feet of Posner with the needle stretched forward like an extension of his arm. One small thrust and he can surely make contact.

"What's in here can kill you. But it works fast and the pain is relatively limited if that makes you feel better." Stern says this knowing that some of the likely reactions are excruciatingly painful, yet it is the doctor in him that now speaks, not the avenger.

"What are you doing? Are you crazy?"

Posner can't help looking down the corridor at the closet and Stern follows his gaze.

"What are you looking for over there? Some kind of help?"

Stern grabs Posner's bicep in a clenched hand. The grip is strong, and Posner winces as he spins around and is pushed down the hall with Stern's other hand holding the syringe.

Posner momentarily thinks Stern might be fooling with the threat, but he can't be sure, and there is no way he can possibly overcome someone as young and athletic as Stern. He allows himself to be steered down the hall. Then he's jerked to a stop.

"What's in here?" Stern waves the needle at the hall closet door.

"Nothing."

"Bullshit. Open it up. Now!"

Posner pulls the door open and then is pushed to the side by Stern's left hand.

"Let's see if it's nothing."

Stern keeps an eye on Posner while he looks into the closet. He switches the needle to his left hand and begins to sweep across the shelves with the other. He snatches various random items from shelves; a blanket, two pillows, a shelf of medicine and cosmetic bottles are all flung across the parquet.

A helpless Posner watches as the bottles slide into a random scatter. He doesn't take his eyes off Stern, but waits for the inevitable when Stern finds the gun. The wait takes seconds, yet his fear never materializes. Stern's free hand stumbles across the box with the Chiefs Special and unknowing its contents sweeps it to the floor. Serendipitously, it lands near Posner's feet as if it was aimed. Before Stern reacts, Posner bends down, opens the box, hoists the revolver and levels it at Stern.

"Drop the needle now. Now!"

Stern's eyes widen as his face seems to shrink into itself like a slow leak in a balloon. His arm drops to his side with the needle pointing straight down. He faces the revolver only feet away, which points straight at his midsection.

Posner holds the gun in his right hand with his left hand supporting the gun wrist. Just like he was taught in his one lesson.

"I said drop it."

The needle slips to the floor.

"Now kick it away."

Stern complies and the needle slides to the far wall.

"That's better. Now let's talk."

Posner's emotions have soared from fear to bravado in less than a minute. The revolver makes him invincible. He sees how a weapon can abolish almost anyone's insecurity. In seconds he's thought through what he will do, but in the end he will kill Stern. The man broke into his home, didn't he? He threatened to kill, didn't he?

Posner steps back a few steps. His gun hand is steady.

"Let me tell you what happened, since you're so interested."

Stern's breathing returns to normal, and if Posner takes the time to look, he will see the man's features fill out as before. Stern's left hand moves a few inches to his side jacket pocket. Posner doesn't notice the movement or the one that follows where Stern pats his pocket and feels the shape of another syringe beneath the flap. His face contorts into something between a smile and a scowl. Posner doesn't notice. He wants to speak. To be in control. It's been so long since he's felt this way. Since before he lost his job.

"You're right. She is dead, but I never had sex with her. If I had maybe everything would be back to normal for all of us, but it's too late. And I didn't kill her. We met on the bus and she talked her way into coming here to see the house. She was pretty pushy about that. As far as sex is concerned, I think she wanted it, but I wasn't interested."

"Sure you weren't."

"No. It's true. It's not that I wasn't tempted, but this is a house I share with my wife. I couldn't do anything. It would have been stupid. I wouldn't have been able to live with myself."

"So she just left and what? Got run over by a car?"

"That's close, but not quite right. You're pretty smart. But then you're a doctor. She told me a lot about you, you know. But if you were so close, then why did she like to see other men?" Posner's sense of invincibility grows with each minute he holds the gun. It's like being God. Able to control life and death. Anything and everything.

Stern looks down. He listens to Posner's words, but doesn't fully process the vocabulary. He hears only what he wants to believe.

"I had to run out to get something and left her here. It took longer than I thought, and when I got back she was lying at the bottom of the stairs. She was dead.

"I first thought she slipped and fell down the stairs. The ones you just walked up. She hit her head and died right there. I know how to check a pulse. There wasn't any. But now I'm not so sure that's what happened. Maybe you followed her on the bus and watched her get in my car and wind up here. Maybe you waited till I left and then came in and killed her. More and more, I think that's what really happened."

Stern doesn't speak. He just lifts his head and begins to shake it sideways in obvious disbelief. Now he begins to pay more attention to the words. His raw anger returns and his face flushes a bright red. Posner still doesn't notice.

"I was scared to explain what happened. I wasn't here when she died. I know it was stupid, but look at the circumstances. A dead woman I never met before in my house. What would the police or my wife think? No. I had to get rid of her body. It's buried out there where you followed me, only a few yards farther away from the gnarled sand pine. You almost found it. Now I can tell the cops where *you* buried her. I'll tell them you told me, or that I followed you to the spot. They'll believe it. It all makes sense. You're their prime suspect, you know. Then they'll be able to close the case."

"Close the case? Why would they do that? It'll only be your word against mine."

"Yeah, but you'll be dead."

Posner doesn't wait for an answer or plea. This is the man who stands in the way of another chance for him and Sara. Sara! He remembers. She could be here any minute. He raises the revolver as Stern puts his hands in front of his body in some surreal misguided attempt at evasion. Posner starts to pull the trigger, but he can't finish. And again, but it's not in him to kill. Then Stern is on him. They collapse into a rotating heap on the floor. The initial impact hammers Posner's skull enough to make him dizzy. They roll into the living room.

The fall jars the revolver loose from Posner's hand and it skips across the floor to the edge of the stairs. Stern scrambles for the gun while Posner half raises himself on two knees and shakes his head to regain clarity. Stern picks up the gun, looks at it, and stuffs it in his inside jacket pocket. He's never held a pistol before and doesn't want to start now. He pulls a needle from another pocket and turns toward Posner but a voice distracts him.

The black Volvo pulls to a stop halfway up the driveway.

"Looks like Amos has a visitor," Ed Whelan says with a nod to the white Chevy as he puts his car into Park.

"Actually, it looks like the Talbots' car, but it can't be. I know they've already left for a few months with their kids in Seattle, but I guess you'll find out soon enough."

"Have a good weekend," adds Frances. "And let us know if you'd like a lift back on Sunday. Just call. Oh, and say a big hi to Amos."

"Will do. And thanks again," answers Sara as she clutches a small duffel and closes the car door. She watches the Volvo slide back into the street, turn, and disappear down the block. She takes a long look at the white Chevrolet parked in the street then mounts the steps. She pulls out her key then hesitates and twists her head a bit toward the ocean only a half block away. She inhales a cool salty breeze and then another before she turns back to the door. The key turns in the lock and the door swings open.

"It's me, Amos. I'm home."

Brigid's Audi brakes just fast enough to make the left turn onto Napeague Lane. Logistics necessitate that she move slower to check for streets and numbers. It doesn't take long. In a few minutes she sees the sign for Posner's street. She starts to make a right, and then stops abruptly as a black Volvo begins a turn out of the same street. A man and woman sit in the front. The man smiles and waves her on. She smiles back. The seconds-long interlude breaks her concentration. The car passes, yet she sits there for several moments. Then she moves forward down the block. There is a blue Lexus parked at the top of Posner's driveway and a white car in the street off to the side. The thought flashes through her mind that if he has visitors, everything may be ruined. The thought passes in seconds.

She pulls into the driveway and looks up just in time to see the front door slam closed as it smothers the sound of a woman's voice. She checks her face in the mirror.

"It's time," she says aloud, swings the door open, slides her legs out of the car, and starts to walk the short distance up the driveway to where the Lexus is parked.

Wisdom puts the overhead on his unmarked Ford sedan as he tries to maneuver his way through East Hampton Village traffic. A few years ago the department resided in a small building closer to the East Hampton–Amagansett border. The newer and larger headquarters sits west of the village. If they hadn't moved, he'd be at Posner's house by now. He checks in with the cruiser, which seems to be as far away as he is, only from the other direction. At last the village falls behind and the road ahead clears. He presses down harder on the gas pedal and the enhanced Ford engine jumps ahead with a surge that pushes him back into his seat.

"Just a few more minutes. Stay where you are, Brigid. I'm coming."

Brigid is about to cross over behind the Lexus when she hears a loud wail from the house. The sound mimics the primal rage of a cornered beast. Whether a man or woman, she can't tell, but she freezes and listens, mouth agape just as the front door flies open. A man races out of the house, trips briefly on the bottom step, recovers almost immediately, and begins a dash down the driveway. He's tall, well over six feet with brown hair. He wears a sports jacket that flaps as he runs. She takes all this in while standing just a few feet from the direct line of his path.

He sees her and skids to sharp stop. His eyes widen and his body shakes.

"Noooooo!" The word escapes him as if he were a wounded animal trapped by hunters in the back of a cave.

"Noooooo!"

One last look. The tortured face of someone beyond hope momentarily faces her. He turns and looks back over his shoulder as if followed by a ghost as he runs to the bottom of the driveway. He enters the white car. In seconds the air fills with the roar of an engine and the shriek of rubber.

It all happens in less than a minute. After the car leaves, she's aware that the howling from within the house hasn't stopped. She hesitates for a moment, then begins to walk quickly up the driveway. That's when she sees a flashing light approach the edge of her vision. No. Two separate sets of lights. Two cars. They arrive within seconds of each other. An official police car parks in the street, and the other car pulls up and stops behind hers.

She watches Wisdom exit the car and face the house. The sounds from inside still wash over them, but now seem more fragmented as if the wailer stops to draw breath every few seconds.

Wisdom motions to the uniform standing by his car some twenty feet below him.

"Stay with her. I'm going inside."

He waits until the uniform arrives before trotting up to the entrance steps. Brigid follows his passage and sees that the front door is slightly ajar. Wisdom draws a pistol from somewhere under his jacket and gently pushes at the door. The volume of the sobs increase as the door swings fully open. She watches Wisdom lower his weapon and step through the doorway. He closes the door behind him and the sound almost disappears as if someone's just turned the radio volume down.

# CHAPTER 20

"Perhaps you'd be more comfortable in your car."

The uniformed policeman is attentive and well spoken.

She thanks him and returns to the Audi. She lights a cigarette and turns the ignition key just enough to be able to open the window halfway down. She pinches a finger and thumb together to pluck an invisible speck of tobacco from her tongue. Another police car arrives followed by an ambulance. Within seconds, yet another car arrives. The driveway is now crowded with police. Two ambulance workers move up to the house together with an equal number of officers. They enter and leave the door open. The wailing sound starts up again for a few moments more and then stops abruptly. She smokes the cigarette down and lights another from the stump of the first. The air suddenly feels chilled. Even surrounded by the police, she feels somehow threatened. She starts the car, closes the window, and adjusts the heater. It is too cool for the pink-and-white dress she wears, and she's embarrassed by her show of cleavage.

After several minutes, she sees Wisdom emerge from the house. He says a few words to a small group of people who replace him. As he walks down the driveway, she leaves her car and meets him.

"What happened in there, Peter?" She's never used his first name before and the familiarity seems to give him momentary pause.

"Posner's wife is dead."

"Dead?" She gasps and staggers backward a step. He reaches out and cups her elbow.

"I'm all right."

"You sure?"

"Yes. What happened?"

"We found her just inside the front door. There was a large needle on the floor under her and Posner was rocking her in his arms. Whatever was in it acted right away. Posner's barely able to talk and the doctor just sedated him. The upstairs is a complete mess. They must have had some fight.

"Did *you* see anything?"

As he speaks, he gestures to a patrolman and makes a scribbling motion with his hand. The officer joins them and pulls out a pad and pen.

"I was in the driveway. Right next to my car. The one over there."

She points to the red Audi, which is conspicuous as the only car in the driveway other than the Lexus amid the crush of police cars.

"This man comes running out of the house. He stops for a moment as he passes me. Shouts something. I think it was, 'No,' then he runs down to his car and drives away."

"Can you describe him?"

"Tall. Like you. Brown hair, I think. Nice looking. Around my age. I think he wore a jacket."

"Did he speak to you?"

"No. I mean other than to scream, 'No' a few times."

"Do you remember the car he drove?"

"No. Only that it was white."

"White?"

"Yes."

"One last question for now. Did you recognize him?"

"No, but I think it must have been Heidi's boyfriend. The doctor."

"Okay. I won't ask you now why you decided to go ahead with the masquerade we originally planned or how you found the address."

"I'm sorry. Herr Weis helped me."

"Of course. Herr Weis. Save us all from diplomats."

He rolls his eyes as he speaks. The message that there's a difference between law enforcement and diplomacy is clear. "Then there's my friend and boss, Sergeant Rick Bennett. You conned him into telling you our local was Posner. Lucky for you that he called me about it right away."

"I'm sorry. I shouldn't have."

"As long as you're okay, but it might have gotten nasty."

"I am truly sorry."

"I said it was okay. And Bennett will be here soon to take over until we can pass it on to County. They handle capital-crime investigations. I'm sure they'll want to interview you."

"I know. Can I go home now? I'm feeling a bit funny."

"Are you all right? Do you need to see a doctor?"

"No. I think I should rest a bit. That's all."

"Do you want me to send an officer with you?"

"No. I'll be fine."

She shakes her head sideways and offers him her hand. He takes it and feels the moisture in her palm. He holds on and looks up. She's breathing rapidly. He can tell by seeing the movement in her chest.

"You'd better go home then and change out of those clothes. It's getting chilly."

She looks down at her dress and folds her arms across her chest.

"Yes. You're right. Thank you again. Goodbye."

"Bye."

Wisdom watches her get back into the Audi and waves two police cars away so she can back out. She raises a hand in thanks and turns down the block. He spends the next several minutes answering questions from various sources. The press arrives, and he asks that they be kept away from the house and that any questions be referred to County. He speaks briefly with Bennett who will be here with a full local team within a few minutes. He walks back to his unmarked sedan at the foot of the driveway, stops, and strokes his chin before he calls a uniformed officer over.

"Drive over to the lady's house in Montauk and be sure everything's okay. Her name is Kashani. Dispatch has her address. It's on Old Montauk Highway. Just past Gurney's Inn."

He watches the uniform drive away in a town cruiser. All he needs to do now is wait for Bennett to take over and find the doctor. He feels badly about Posner and his wife. He should have done more to warn him. Maybe he should have been there himself after he found out that Stern was hanging around.

But at least Brigid's safe.

# CHAPTER 21

The car sprints to seventy-five in seconds. Stern's hands squeeze the wheel in unconcealed fury. The Chevrolet flies down the eastbound highway toward Montauk.

"No. It wasn't her. She's dead." He repeats the words over and over. The road ahead is clear, yet all he sees beyond the windshield is Heidi in the pink-and-white dress. Why didn't he stop when he saw her standing there? But maybe she wasn't there. What if it's all in his mind? Maybe she's out there buried in the Montauk Overlook like Posner said.

But what if he was just lying to torture me? What if she's not dead at all? Maybe she's been living here with him all this time.

"The bitch! I'll kill her. Right now. Today. The bitch!"

The car brakes with such suddenness that it skids into a double spin and comes to rest in the opposite breakdown lane of the momentarily deserted stretch of highway. He sits back and gasps. It could have been all over right there. No. He was spared because he still had one more urgent thing to do. But how?

"Concentrate! Think! Think!"

The answer, he realizes, rests back where he just came from. He reaches into his jacket pocket and removes the pistol he took from Posner. This will have to do. There are no more insulin syringes. He examines the weapon for the first time and becomes aware of its smoothness. The weight is less than he thought it would be. Probably no more than a few pounds. Why was Posner unable to pull the trigger? Stupid bastard either didn't have the brains to cock the gun, or the balls to shoot it. If he had, I wouldn't be sitting here. I'd be dead and not that woman.

In some way it's Posner's own fault that woman's dead. Who was she? His wife? Another girlfriend? Too bad he didn't get to see her and Heidi meet up. That would have been some catfight. Heidi's tough. He's seen it a hundred times. But that other woman? That's just a coincidental accident. What the army calls collateral damage. Hell, when he heard her voice all he could think of was getting out of there. He would have too, and she'd be alive, if he hadn't tripped on the last steps and skidded into her with the needle.

It's too bad, but he doesn't feel sorry. He laughs aloud. Posner got what he deserved for being so stupid. He hefts the gun. He needs to be sure it will work. He looks down both sides of the road. He's still alone. He points the gun into the passenger seat cushion and squeezes.

The roar is deafening despite the muffling effect of the cushion. There is also a recoil he doesn't expect, but the mechanism works. He spins the barrel and sees four bullets left. More than enough. He returns the revolver to his coat pocket. The motor is still running, and he eases the car back onto the road and begins to drive back toward Posner's neighborhood. He stays at the speed limit and exits a few blocks from the Posner turnoff, drives to a nearby beach access, and sits with the engine off. He must wait a bit more. He knows it. So he sits and watches the ocean, but after only ten minutes he needs to get going again.

He leaves the beach and swings the car around an extra few blocks to avoid being seen from Posner's home and approaches the house he's stayed in from the other direction. Just as he cuts into the driveway, the flashing lights from down the block at Posner's house catch his eye. It's only for a moment through, as the garage door is already in motion and daylight disappears in seconds.

The same bedroom window he's used before still offers an unobstructed view of the Posner house. Rotating ambulance and police lights fill that end of the street. There's only one ambulance and he watches two medics wheel a gurney and stretcher up the driveway. The medics lift the stretcher and carry it inside. Four police cars line the street and a fifth arrives as he watches.

There's a large crowd of people milling around. Most are in police uniforms. He also sees Wisdom in pants and jacket and a few men in suits. People enter and leave the house in a steady flow. He sees a pink-and-white dress appear from behind a parked car.

It's her, the bitch. She's alive. The bitch. He curses as he watches her move towards a police car. Wisdom walks over to her, speaks for a moment, and then calls a policeman over. She and Wisdom speak and the policeman listens and writes on a pad. They seem to finish and talk for only a few more seconds then shake hands. She moves her head sideways. She's turning him down.

"What for? Does he want some too? Didn't think you turned anyone down."

She gets into a red Audi. There are two police cars behind her and she clearly must wait while they pull back. It gives him time. He races back to the garage and into the Chevy. The automatic door rolls opens. The street at his end of the block is still empty. He pulls to the edge of the driveway and watches as she pulls away and turns the corner. He rolls his car into the road and speeds up going down the adjacent block. He should catch up with her in a minute or two. It's hard to lose a red car.

# CHAPTER 22

Wisdom is officially out of the picture the moment the Suffolk County Police Department takes over. Still, Bennett is close to the County people and keeps him advised of the case's status. An all out search is on, but by evening there's no immediate sign of Stern.

"He's gone to ground somewhere," Bennett notes, acknowledging the obvious. "We also found out something about his past that we never knew. Seems that when he was in his teens living upstate, he threatened to kill some girl who publicly humiliated him. A few hours later she was found dead in a car accident. The police investigated, but no charges were ever filed. The inquiry is public knowledge. The info came from the archives of a local paper, the *Berkshire Eagle.*"

"That shows zilch, except that maybe he didn't like girls who gave him a hard time."

"Exactly. It also covers every guy who ever lost out with someone they fancied."

"Anything official yet from the County Medical Examiner's Office?"

"No surprises. The County ME says that the preliminary result is that Sara Posner died from a lethal injection of insulin. She went into shock and died within a few minutes. It must have been rough shit for Posner. Holding her there while she convulsed then dies and unable to do anything."

"I should have known when I went inside. I should have spotted it. I've seen insulin shock before."

"It was already too late when you got there. And why should you have assumed it was insulin shock? She could have been unconscious for a dozen reasons. And remember, no one even found the needle until after the EMTs picked her up because she fell on top of it at some point.

"We did find another needle upstairs. It was full to the brim with insulin, but unused. It was lying on the floor almost hidden amongst a pile of bottles, towels, and whatever. You name it. Stern must have dropped it when he and Posner fought. It's the only possibility, but we'll confirm it when we speak to Posner."

"So Stern came prepared to kill at least once and maybe again."

"How's Posner?"

"He's at Southampton Hospital. Doc says maybe County can speak to him this evening. You're welcome to join them. Unofficially, of course."

"I'd like that. Thanks, but I'm just too busy."

"Then I'll fill you in later. Okay if I call?"

"That'll work. I'll be here till at least eight."

"What about the sister?"

"As far as I know she's okay, although she was pretty shook up. I haven't seen or spoken to her since this afternoon, but I think she'll probably be leaving to go back to Geneva in a few days. I did have a cruiser check in on her just to be safe, but she told the uniform not to bother her. Said she'd be all right on her own. I believe she can handle it, but I'll still have someone watch the house until we find this guy."

"That's good. I shouldn't have confirmed Posner's location. It was stupid and unprofessional."

The comment surprises Wisdom. It is rare for Bennett to second guess any of his actions.

"Not true. She just conned you good. Probably in the genes. Her sister, Heidi, must have been even better."

"Yeah, and look where it got her."

✦ ✦ ✦

At eight fifteen that evening, Wisdom's cell phone rings. He's hoping it's Bennett and it is.

"Well, Posner's still in a bad way and likely to be that way for a while. They plan to ease up on his sedation, but looks like they'll keep him on it for at least another day or two."

"Any family to help out?"

"Nothing here. She has relatives in Phoenix. We'll contact them through local channels. He's not yet up to anything like that. NYPD checked with her law firm in the city, but no one was that close. Or at least admitted to it."

"What's that supposed to mean?"

"Only that some staffers thought she might have strayed off the ranch. But it might only have been office gossip. After all, they did live apart some of the time."

"This is getting too complicated. What did Posner say?"

"Okay. Just let me smooth out my notes. We did have a stenographer there, so this is the quick-and-dirty version."

"Go ahead."

"To start with, Stern knocks and Posner lets him in."

"Just like that?"

"Yes. That's what he said. Told us he was expecting his wife, or even thought it might be you, since you'd called him earlier. Said Stern just walked in, went up the stairs, and began to threaten him. Accused Posner of having sex with Heidi, and then killing her. After Posner denies the whole thing, Stern pulls out this needle. Doesn't tell Posner what's in it, only that it could kill him. Posner tries to go down the hall to a closet where they keep a loaded gun. There's a valid permit. It's a relic from his wife's brief career as a judge in Queens. Anyway, he doesn't get there in time and they struggle. Stern drops the needle in the fight. That's when Posner hits his head and winds up with the bloody scalp you saw."

"So when did the wife get involved?"

"After Posner falls down and hits his head, Stern pulls another needle out of his pocket. Posner thinks he's gonna come at him again when the wife walks in."

"And?"

"And Stern decides to leave and runs down the steps. Posner sees all this from his spot on the floor near the top of the stairs. His wife has just come inside the front door when Stern tumbles into her with the needle. Then he's gone. Runs by your friend Brigid in the driveway and a few minutes later you show up."

"Could it have been an accident? I mean, sticking the wife."

"Could have been, but we both know that if you show up with a lethal weapon and it causes a death, you're still responsible. Anyway, I wouldn't be surprised if Posner revises this sometime later. He was pretty messed up when we spoke."

There's a pause. Wisdom has an uncanny feeling that both he and Bennett are having the same thoughts about distraught survivors. They both have a history of speaking to people who've overcome big time trauma. It's never easy. It's never what he thought about before going on the job. Sometimes there's very little to say. He remembers seeing Posner rock his wife in his arms. He remembers how the poor son of a bitch struggled to keep the medics from taking her away. What could he have said to the man at that moment that would make a difference? But he did say something. He had to. Words of comfort that probably didn't register but were still necessary. It's important for people to know that they're not alone, that someone else cares, however lame it might sound.

Wisdom breaks into the silence. "Did he see what kind of car Stern came in?"

"No."

"Okay then. We'll have to work with Brigid's visual description of a white car. Did he say anything else?"

“One thing. I wrote it down to get it straight even without waiting for the transcript.”

Wisdom hears the rustle of paper over his cell phone.

“Posner said that, ‘Stern has the gun. He took it with him.’ They’re his exact words. ‘Stern has the gun.’ ”

“Wonderful. Just fucking wonderful.”

# CHAPTER 23

He shouldn't be driving the Chevy. Someone might have seen it, but he isn't worried. In just a short bit of time he expects to have Heidi's shiny Audi to drive. She's up ahead about a hundred yards farther down the road. The highway is flat and empty. A red Audi makes an easy target to follow despite the fading afternoon light that sends a shadow creeping halfway across the road.

When the highway splits, she takes the right-hand fork onto Old Montauk Highway. In a moment he's riding amidst a network of short blind hills and curves. He needs to slow down, so he takes the risk and brakes, hoping he won't lose her even though he'll fall farther behind. He passes Gurney's Inn to his right on the side that faces the ocean just as he picks up her rear bumper gliding around another turn. When he comes to the top of yet another hill, he sees a flash of red as she pulls a sharp right off the road into a crushed-stone driveway.

He eases off the gas and coasts past the house just as he sees the car disappear around the side. He assumes she parks in back or in a hidden garage. He drives farther along the hilly road for another fifty yards until he finds what seems to be a deserted driveway. He parks behind a clump of trees and begins to walk back up the road.

He's no more than thirty feet from her driveway entrance when he sees a police car coming from the other direction. He slips behind a wall of privet and watches as the white cruiser boldly inscribed with POLICE in blue letters moves into her driveway. The police car stops in front. A tall muscular cop exits and moves to the main entrance. The man's size is enough for Stern to unconsciously move a few feet farther back.

He sees Heidi open the door. She's still dressed in pink and white, but from his position behind a hedge, she somehow looks different. He's not sure why and moves closer, now more confident in his ability to remain unobserved. The cop speaks and she answers. The whole conversation takes no more than thirty seconds. It ends as she shakes her head sideways and closes the door. Stern monitors the policeman as the man reenters his car and drives off back in the direction of Amagansett.

He waits another five minutes, and then goes back to the Chevy. He turns it around and follows the main road until it reaches Heidi's driveway. He turns in and continues around to the back where he sees the red Audi and parallel parks a few feet away. When he's sure he's not visible from the road, he cuts the engine. He pulls the revolver from his pocket as he walks around to the front door.

"Guess who's coming, Heidi?"

He speaks into the growing darkness, but a slight gust of wind rustles the pines and keeps any sound from the house. He becomes anxious. More than usual. Even more than at Posner's house. From the space in front of her entrance door, he checks the road. There are no sounds; even the birds have given up their chatter for the day. One last spear of light glimmers through a far cluster of trees before it too moves on and plunges the house into night. So quick, he wonders. Almost too quick. He knocks twice, waits a few seconds, and then raps again. A voice calls out from inside, thought the words are indistinct.

"It's the police again. Sorry, we forgot something. It'll only take a minute." He smiles to himself at the calmness of his voice. I must even sound like a cop, he muses, but there's no time to dwell on his impersonation.

The door opens. She still wears the pink-and-white dress. From this close he sees that she looks very different. He levels the pistol at her, pushes the door open wide, and steps inside.

"Remember me?"

He stops speaking and studies her again. Now he's less than two feet away. The hair looks pretty much the same and the body wrapped in the familiar dress is just as sexy as he remembered, but the overall effect he sees is that of a different person. This Heidi is slightly taller. The big difference though is in the face. It is definitely familiar, but it's not Heidi's. The eyes are just as black and the skin tone is just as olive, but the nose is too long and the bump in the middle is gone. He breathes deeply, and his eyes flutter closed for a moment before he rubs them with his free hand.

"No. You wouldn't remember me. I'm the man who fucked Heidi for over a year, but I've never fucked you. At least not yet. So who the hell are you?"

There is no answer, just a short intake hiss as the woman gasps for breath. He enters the house and slams the door.

"Where's the bedroom?" His words fly out like a fist.

She doesn't answer and seems to struggle to stay upright. Her face pales in contrast to the olive complexion of her arms. He spins her around just as he sees her legs begin to shake. He pushes her forward. She stumbles across the room and stops when one hand grabs the door jamb at the edge of a long corridor. He drags her away and moves down the empty corridor, but this time he pulls at her arm rather than pushing at her back. He stops at the first room with a light, a bedroom.

"This should do. Is it yours?" His voice trembles with anticipation. One hand holds her against the wall and the other waves the gun in a small overhead circle.

"Ja." She speaks for the first time and half raises one hand to point into the room.

The room is painted a light blue. The only light comes from a single lamp that rests alone on a small table adjacent to a queen-sized bed that's crowned with a light-colored wood headboard. There is no spread and the pillows are fluffed and the blanket turned down. A small dresser of similar wood occupies the opposite wall. Its surface is empty except for a television that plays an old movie with token volume. Dark curtains are drawn across the only windows.

He pushes her across the room. She lurches to the bed and crumples at the edge. One hand reaches out and clutches a pillow to her chest.

No. She isn't Heidi.

"Who are you? I won't ask again."

She fails to react. His words fall on a woman paralyzed by fear. Paralysis makes him thinks of another chemical he almost used for Posner, the tropical poison curare. It works like deadly snake venom and leaves its victims paralyzed and unable to breathe. He will make her talk though. It's easy enough.

"Take your clothes off!"

She pulls the pillow tighter across her chest, but he moves forward and pulls it away.

"I said take off your clothes! Now!"

She looks around as if help could be found somewhere in the sparse room, but the only diversion from her fear is a nearly soundless Cary Grant on the television. She looks at Stern again.

"I'm Heidi's sister, Brigid."

"She doesn't have a sister. She would have told me."

"We had a big fight several years ago."

"Later," he says. "Tell me all about it later."

He is no longer listening, just staring. Now she's Heidi again, not Brigid or whoever. The face and body morph back into the woman he knows. The woman he thought he'd lost. But she's back now. It's not a great leap to have Heidi back again.

He takes off his jacket and drops it on the dresser next to the television. Then he puts his gun on top of the jacket. When he speaks again his voice is very different, softer, and even tender.

"Get undressed, Heidi. You know you want to. It's what you always want."

She stands from the bed with effort and one trembling arm stretches behind for the zipper. He stares for a moment longer, tastes a sudden dryness in his mouth, and then begins to unbutton his shirt.

# CHAPTER 24

Wisdom knows that with their current information, it'll be no problem for the Suffolk County Police to get NYPD's help in getting a warrant to search Stern's New York apartment. Stern is now officially a fugitive. The day has passed, however, without a sign of the man.

At a quarter to nine on the morning after the events at Posner's house, Bennett calls Wisdom with preliminary results. Except for a few hours of troubled sleep, Wisdom hasn't left his desk since he got back from Posner's house. Brigid is back at her house and Posner is at Southampton Hospital for observation. The County police are in charge now, yet Wisdom won't let it rest until they clear it all up, not with Stern still running around. He grabs for the phone and comes perilously close to knocking over a nearly full cup of coffee in the process, even though a few splashes fly across his desk. Bennett ignores Wisdom's curses and plunges ahead.

"Two things of interest: one, he had another six needles of insulin in his apartment fridge. The man could have been his own lethal-weapon machine, especially since his official hospital medical records show no evidence of diabetes."

"And the other?"

"We found some unusual pills in his medicine cabinet. Notably a nearly full bottle of something called Seroquel."

"What?"

"Seroquel. It's apparently an antipsychotic drug prescribed for schizophrenia."

"God. This is getting messier. Who's the prescribing doctor?"

"He is. The hospital may have suspended him, but he still has his license. That's why he can still prescribe. For himself or anyone else. That's how he got the insulin. The needles were still in a bag with the pharmacy name on it."

Wisdom questions aloud what other prescription medications Stern's helped himself to.

"We'll have a list of all other drugs he's ordered either to self-medicate or otherwise in a few more hours, at least from that pharmacy."

"Okay and thanks for keeping me in the loop."

His last words disappear into Bennett's dial tone.

"So the doctor is psychotic." His words tumble out and roll over a silent audience.

Wisdom pulls up the Internet on his screen and starts to research mental illnesses. Police work provides a broad education beyond the law. Wisdom has a general fragmentary knowledge of many medical issues, but is probably less informed about mental health matters than anything else. He could call the department psychologist, but first opts for a quick check of the web. He finds a site with the heading, "An Introduction to Schizophrenia." He opens it and begins to read, but almost as quickly has a chilling thought. Heidi used to be a resident in psychiatry, and now that her ex-lover might well need her professional help, it's too late. A mental postscript forces him to wonder whether Heidi ever knew Stern had such a problem.

The details go on for pages and there's no end to the links available to other websites on the subject, but in twenty minutes he manages to absorb some basic essentials. A blurred distinction between truth and fantasy jumps out at him. A person might behave in a very normal fashion one moment, and then switch seamlessly into an entirely different person where a wide range of abnormal behavior is possible. Some references are to split personalities and there are many cases on record of multiple personalities in the same individual, each waiting for some trigger to release them. A person could curse, cry, hallucinate, and in general depart from normal human interaction in an instant. Violent behavior is possible. One of the medical treatments mentioned includes the drug Seroquel, the one found in Stern's apartment.

Wisdom leans back and focuses his eyes on a square white ceiling tile. If Stern needs Seroquel, it's very likely that he may suffer from hallucinations, and if so, then what would he have thought when he caught a quick glimpse of Brigid in Posner's driveway, looking for the entire world like the Heidi in his memory? How would a troubled mind react to seeing his presumed dead lover turn up alive and as beautiful as he remembered? Maybe it wouldn't mean much if he was on his meds, but they did find the mostly filled pill bottle in his apartment, didn't they? If he's off the meds, then he could really be off-the-wall.

His thoughts are interrupted by another call from Bennett.

"Got some more interesting news for you. After Brigid told us about Stern having a white car we checked registrations for white cars against local addresses. Seems the people down the block who live in a house on the far corner of Posner's street have a white Chevy Malibu. And get this. It's the same location where Stern's cell phone calls were made. Only he wasn't standing outside when he made them. He was in the house. A team just got back from there. No white Chevy, but Stern's rented Ford is in the garage. And one more thing. There's plenty of evidence that the guy spent time upstairs, and from the bedroom window he'd have a clear view of anyone around Posner's house."

"Meaning?"

"Meaning he could have doubled back and watched everything going on from his cozy little window seat. He could have seen all of us come and go as well."

"Including Brigid. He could have seen Brigid."

"Right. And he could have followed her back to her house. When did she leave Posner's? Late afternoon?"

"That's it. But I had a cruiser stop by after she got home as well as this morning. Everything seemed quiet."

"Did patrol speak to her?"

"Yes. Yesterday as well as this morning. Everything seemed normal and quiet."

"I wouldn't trust quiet in a case like this."

"Roger that. I'm on it."

He presses another button to dial the patrol dispatcher and asks them to patch him through to the cruiser that checked out Brigid's house that morning.

"It was exactly eight-o-five when I knocked on the door. I'm reading right off my book."

"Anything unusual?"

"Nothing I could see. Oh, she did take more than a few minutes to answer the door. Said she was sleeping. And she was wearing that same dress that she had on the day before. You know, the pink and white one."

"I know," agrees Wisdom, but a bell goes off. Why would she be still wearing the dress she claims she dislikes so much on the next day? Or, for that matter, even a minute longer than she ever needed to?

"Anything else? Did she say there was any problem?"

"No. Said everything was fine. Thanked me and said goodbye."

At that moment Wisdom's mind starts to wander and his silence is obvious.

"Anything else, sir?"

"No. that's all. Thanks. Unless you can think of something else."

"Well there's one thing. Maybe it's nothing, but all the time we spoke, and it couldn't have been for more than half a minute, she kept rubbing her wrists. Alternating hands."

"Like to get the circulation going?"

"Right. Like someone just took the cuffs off. We've sure seen it enough to know the motion."

"Holy shit! He's there. He's with her. He's holding her hostage. Where are you now?"

"Montauk village."

"You're a good ten minutes closer than me. Get over there right away but stay on the main road away from the driveway until I get there. I'll call in for backup. No one in or out.

"And pass the word that I'm driving over there and should make it in about twenty minutes."

He disconnects and jumps out of his chair. In the process he knocks the rest of his already cold coffee off the desk and onto the floor. He snatches his jacket, hops over a puddle, and races out the door. The wall clock he passes in the hall reads a minute before ten.

He presses the gas pedal halfway to the floor and sticks the overhead on the roof. Just enough time to call Bennett, who'll get onto County. He doesn't care who gets the collar. After all the mistakes he's made, starting with his agreeing to the pink-and-white dress masquerade, he just wants Brigid to be safe. He sees the Old Montauk Highway fork and veers to the right. He risks keeping the speed at fifty despite the blind hills.

"Hang in there, Brigid. I'm coming. I'm coming."

Even though he's alone in the car and still a few miles from her house, he still hopes she can somehow hear him.

# CHAPTER 25

The next morning arrives with shafts of sunlight that steal around the curtains and outline Brigid's rigid body as it lays spread across the white duvet cover. Her eyes are shut, legs splayed apart, as if posed in a men's magazine, but there's no overt eroticism. Her arms stretch above her head where the wrists are tied to bedposts with her own stockings. A shallow breathing betrays the only sign of life. The only clothing is a white bra and matching cotton panties. No thongs in her life, Stern thinks. Not like Heidi who sought the prospect of sexuality in every garment. The plainness and simplicity of the underwear actually desexualized the woman, although he knows it's more than that

He studies her body again. Her breasts seem smaller when she lies flat and the few tiny black curls that escape the underwear are the only hints at what might have propelled him into a state of erotic arousal, only it didn't work. Nothing worked.

He remembers the previous night. She lay there just as she does now. He'd tied her arms and she began to cry, which he blatantly ignored. He removed his own shirt, pants, shoes, and socks. He hooked his fingers into the elastic of his Jockey shorts and then stopped. Nothing happened. He wanted to fuck this woman out of anger, yet nothing happened. He stroked himself, but arousal still eluded him. She watched him for a moment then averted her eyes.

Just like with Heidi, he remembers. Maybe she really is Heidi. He isn't sure whether he speaks or thinks the words. Logic tells him it's the fucking Seroquel. He started taking the pills randomly again a few weeks ago from the old bottle, but the results are mixed. Sometimes he feels calmer, yet he still imagines things. Sometimes he still feels like he's in another person's body. Half of him wants to believe Heidi's still alive. The other side to the medication is that it depresses his sexual desire to the point of nonexistence. He accepts now that he's in some kind of sexual twilight zone, where relatively normal social behavior can arrive at the risk of losing all sexual drive. Conversely, if his old sexual appetites return, he assumes it will be at the cost of more serious mental disorders. He clinically dissects his condition, as he always has, mentally adding up the gains and losses of any approach. Sometimes he makes the wrong choice, just as with a patient. Last night he was determined to fuck this woman's brains out but couldn't even get semihard. In the end he tied her up and fled to the living room couch, but sleep joined sexual performance as elusive goals.

When he heard her calling, "*Bitte,* toilet, toilet, *bitte,* please," sometime during the night, he went in to untie the knots so she could use the bathroom. Then he positioned her as before and at that time felt even less aroused than he had earlier.

His watch shows eight and she looks as if she's still sleeping, but he guesses she's only faking it. Like she faked being Heidi yesterday. Her whole story is just so much bullshit.

He puts on his jacket and drops the gun into a side pocket outside of the flap.

"Time to get up, sleepyhead," he says and loosens the stocking around her right wrist.

He's just starting to untie her second wrist when he hears a knock at the door. There's a moment of paralysis when everything he's ever feared in his life leaps out at him; his father's endless stream of disapprovals, anxiety over possible rejection by girls, passing the MCATs, loss of Heidi's affection, and now the police. He shakes her into a wakefulness he knew was there all the time. Her eyes are open and alert.

"Get dressed." He throws her the same pink-and-white dress.

"Get up! Now! Someone's here." His words are bookended by another round of raps at the front door.

She scrambles into the dress, staggers across the room and then down the corridor as she rubs her wrists with alternate hands.

"Not a word," he tells her in a hoarse whisper. "Or I'll kill you and whoever else is there."

He hoists the gun above his head to be sure she sees it and waits at the edge of the corridor where he can see both her and the front door, yet stay unobserved.

"*Ja*. Yes."

"Police."

She opens the door. From his hidden position, Stern sees that the zipper on the back of her dress is half open and she's not wearing shoes, but the cop won't see anything unusual. Overall, she'll appear as normal as anyone who's just woken up.

"Morning, ma'am. Just checking in to see how you're doing."

"I'm fine. I just got up. Sorry it took so long to answer the door."

"That's okay. Sure everything's fine?"

"Quite sure, thank you. Goodbye then and thank you for stopping by."

Stern pictures the cop tip his hat as the door closes. He waits until he hears the engine cough its way into smoothness, and then ten seconds more before he checks the front window just in time to watch the taillights turn out of her driveway and onto the main road.

"Too many cops around here. We need to leave," he tells her in a matter-of-fact way as they walk back down the corridor toward the bedroom. A distant observer might think they were discussing a movie date or details for a picnic rather than a life-threatening circumstance.

"Put enough things for a few days in a small bag and be ready in ten minutes."

He doesn't know why he says this, and then realizes he does it to make her think it's all just temporary, and that in a few days everything will revert to normal. She does seem calmer at this point, and he assumes his ruse will work. He also senses a kind of serenity working its way through his own body. This is the upside. If he can't get it up, at least he can begin to act like a normal person. He's already glad he didn't force himself on her last night.

She takes a few items from a top dresser drawer and turns to him.

"Where are we going?"

"Not far," he answers as his mind impels an image of a gnarled sand pine and the ground beneath it. "Not far at all."

# CHAPTER 26

She begins to relax as soon as he agrees to let her change into pants and a sweater. They take the Audi and he drives. As soon as they're on the main road heading east toward Montauk village, he glances sideways at her.

"You don't look like her at all anymore."

"It was the dress. I was supposed to wear the dress to fool you and the other person."

"You mean Posner?"

"Yes."

"He did it you know. He killed Heidi and buried her. That's where we're going now. To where she is. To be sure."

"How do you know he killed her?"

This time Stern steals a longer look but keeps driving. He is no longer the wild person she remembers from yesterday. Maybe he's taken some medication. Maybe he realizes she's not a threat.

"He told me so. Oh, he first gave me some bullshit story that she had an accident in his house while he was out, and then when he came home and found her he got scared and buried her. But he killed her. Either he raped her or he tried and killed her when she resisted. He killed her all right.

"Second, and most important, I know I didn't do it. I loved her. I still do."

He pauses and she sees one eye begin to well up. He makes no move to wipe it.

"I know that. She told me."

"She told you? When? What did she say?"

He doesn't wait for an answer. They are nearly through the village of Montauk when he makes a sharp turn onto South Edison Street. He drives until the street ends and pulls into a small stretch of alley behind two shuttered seasonal motels, and then stops. A dumpster blocks any cursory view from the road. There is a narrow sliver of beach and ocean through the front windshield. He turns the engine off and leans back.

"I have to rest. Too tired. Need to rest for a bit."

She says nothing. After a minute he leans forward and pulls out a packet of Winstons and offers her one. She accepts and he lights them both up. The digital clock on the dash flashes 9:44 as he puts the lighter back.

"Now tell me. Please."

She looks around at the quiet space they sit in and then back at him.

"Don't be afraid anymore."

She looks at him, sees the earnestness of a teenager, and begins to relax.

"Now tell me everything she said. "

# CHAPTER 27

Wisdom parks behind the cruiser that waits on the road apron some fifty feet west of Brigid's driveway. In less than a minute, two more blue-and-whites appear. Wisdom directs them to park on the east side of the driveway. He sends two men to cover the road access and two more to the rear of the house.

"No one in or out. SOP." They all voice agreement. Logistics aren't an issue. They've all been trained.

Wisdom walks down the driveway to the front door, which is slightly ajar. He identifies himself and slowly pushes the door open. He turns and calls for one of the uniforms to join him.

He advises the men in the back by radio to stay on the outside.

"Anything moving back there?" he asks.

"Negative. But there is a car parked here."

"What make?"

"White Chevy Malibu. Two years old."

"Stay where you are. We're going in."

"Ten-four."

Even as he pulls the Glock from his holster belt, Wisdom wonders about Brigid's red Audi. Is it parked in a garage somewhere in back or is she gone? Gone with Stern?

He moves forward into the house and announces his presence. Police presence. There's no answer. They cover every room. The house is immaculate except for one bedroom. A bed is messed up and two nylon stockings lay discarded across a pillow. The pink-and-white dress is on the floor. He asks one of the uniforms to pack it up together with the nylons.

The search is futile. The house is empty. There is no Audi. No obvious clues as to where she might have gone. Wisdom returns to his car and calls in. He decides to leave two uniforms at the house and passes instructions to get the plate number on the rented Audi. A call to Weis confirms that it's from a local Audi dealer. Shouldn't take long. As soon as they confirm the plate, every cruiser in the area will be alerted with an APB.

He sits in his car after passing out instructions. Frustration overwhelms him. His anger is directed internally more than anything else. It's all his fault. He should have protected Posner. If he had, Posner's wife would still be alive. He shouldn't have gotten involved with Brigid's masquerade idea. He should have picked up Stern earlier. All the things he should or shouldn't have done. All the things he's fucked up just on this one case.

A call from Bennett shakes him back. Yes, Bennett had already heard about Stern and Brigid. But he has something new. Posner called. He wants to speak to both of them. Has something important to say, but wants them all to meet at the house. His house in Amagansett.

"I thought he was sedated and in the hospital."

"He was, but won't take any more pills. He sounded pretty lucid considering everything that's gone down. Insists he needs to talk to us. He specifically mentioned that he wants you there. Seems like a man who desperately needs to get something off his chest, even if part of him is falling apart. I spoke to the doctor who confirms he's okay to travel, at least physically."

"When?"

"As soon as we can all get there. He's still in Southampton Hospital. I'll pick him up and meet you at his house."

"Okay. I'm on the way. Right now I can't do anything more here."

✦ ✦ ✦

Southampton Hospital has no formal psychiatric ward, or other comparable isolation area, so Posner is placed in a private intensive-care room as soon as he arrives, which is about six that evening. Sedation does little to halt his spasms of grief. At first he cannot believe what's happened. He lies in bed and asks over and over for Sara. A doctor checks the laceration on his scalp and pronounces it minor. Nurses enter and leave. One shakes her head and disappears without comment, yet he knows. Bit by bit he remembers and knows she's gone. The crying then begins with hysterical ferocity, yet after a few hours the worst passes. He is left with nothing except an overwhelming emptiness, a numbness he feels will never pass.

He declines an offer to speak with a local clergyman, but allows a staff psychologist a few minutes. It helps a bit and he begins to calm. He's told that the police wish to speak with him and agrees to meet with them early the next day.

At seven the next morning Detective Bennett and Detective Cooper from the County police together with a stenographer come to sit with him. He has declined any more tranquilizers, yet fights to put aside what happened. He begins to speak, but his recall is interrupted more than once by convulsive sobs. He can't help himself. He manages to tell them about the confrontation and Stern's threat to kill him. He describes the fight, but only speaks minimally of the part when Stern runs out and Sara dies. He omits the period where he tells Stern about finding a dead Heidi and burying her. It is as if that part never happened.

After they leave, he realizes it's still not enough. He can't roll back time. He needs to tell a different story. Sara is gone. His mind gains a renewed clarity. He has to punish Stern. Otherwise nothing would have happened. It's the only way to preserve Sara's memory and what they would have had together. That's all he has left. He could never admit now that he disposed of Heidi's body. That might detract from Stern's guilt and he needs to make sure they know Stern killed Heidi.

He sees how it must have happened. Stern watched Heidi board the bus in the city and followed it to the East End of Long Island. He parked in East Hampton and trailed her as she walked around the village until she entered my car. He saw them go into the house. He waited outside while his mind imagined the worst, and then when he saw me leave, he entered the house. He killed Heidi and left with the body before I returned. Yes. That's how it happened. There was no accident.

He needs to talk to the police again. He'll tell them he knows where Stern buried her. They'll believe him. Why not? And it's all for Sara, isn't it? He calls for a nurse and asks her to send Bennett a message.

Bennett picks up Posner from the hospital shortly before noon the next day. Sara Posner has been dead for less than twenty-four hours. Posner wears the same clothes he had on from the day before. The hospital identification band still circles his left wrist. He's neither shaved nor tried to comb his hair. He sits in the backseat and says nothing, nor does Bennett speak to him after the car pulls out. Detective Cooper from County sits in the front alongside Bennett. They drive for twenty minutes in silence except for Posner's periodic whimpering spurts.

Wisdom meets them at the front step. He has been there for some time. A uniform has already cut the yellow crime-scene tape and removed the door seal. Wisdom goes in first, together with Cooper, and they both move up the stairs. At the top, Wisdom turns and sees Posner and Bennett as they stand just inside the front door. Posner starts to talk, but his speech is fragmented and disjointed to the point where Wisdom thinks the man is about to unravel in front of his eyes. He is almost afraid to watch as Posner stands in the spot where his wife died and begins mumbling bits of incoherence.

"Everything's here. Right here. At this place. In this spot. Everything. Right here. Here."

Posner stops abruptly. Shoulders begin to heave just before his body explodes into sobs.

More than a minute passes before Bennett helps him up the steps. They sit on facing couches with Bennett alongside Posner. More time passes and Wisdom watches as Posner's grief shifts to a gentle weeping. He is a step closer to calm. Bennett offers a glass of water, but Posner points to an open bottle of Merlot on the credenza. Bennett pours him a generous glassful. Posner drinks avidly, and then turns slightly so that he can see all three men. He sniffles twice and begins to speak. His voice is surprisingly clear, but the pain is there, carved into his features. Wisdom and Bennett make quick eye contact. Cooper barely blinks. Such pain never dissipates quickly, if ever. They've all seen it before.

"At first I didn't want to get him, I mean Stern, in trouble. I didn't tell you the whole truth about that day I saw the blue car following me when I drove to Montauk village."

"What happened?" Cooper does the talking. Bennett listens and Wisdom has his notepad ready.

"After the blue car went past me, I followed it beyond the village until it turned off."

"Where was that?"

"At the Montauk Overlook. When I got there, he had just left the car and was walking into the woods. I slowed down enough to see him stop by a bent sand pine. Then I drove off quickly without stopping again, but I'm pretty sure it was him. Stern."

"Can you show us the spot? I mean, right now." Bennett's tone shows his own concern.

Posner nods. Wisdom guesses that if the man tries to speak anymore, his voice might dissolve into inaudibility. Wisdom calls ahead to have backup meet them at the traffic circle in Montauk village. Cooper uses his cell and confirms that County will send two more of their own cars.

Wisdom has a strong hunch. Despite the man's instability, he's convinced Stern hasn't run away. He feels that Stern is somehow compelled to bring Brigid to the spot where he buried Heidi, perhaps as an act of confession, but who knows what someone in his mental state might do. Wisdom's intuition is well respected and he convinces Bennett and Cooper that Stern and Brigid might be there. All he can do now is hope that he's right, and that she's still okay by the time they arrive.

# CHAPTER 28

They sit in the parked car and she decides to lie, or at least say what she thinks Heidi would say, or more to the point, what Stern would like to hear her say. Stern seems to be warming to the prospect of hearing good words about himself from Heidi. Brigid looks over at him as he leans against the driver-side window. He appears like a beaten man. He's actually quite handsome if he were to shave off his stubble and comb his hair. She could see why Heidi would have been attracted to him. Still, he does look trampled in some way. Flattened by sad events and unfilled needs; a duo she knows intimately. He looks as if he needs sleep and confirms this as he yawns without stop and rubs at his eyes. She's also tired. It's time for her to deliver and hope it's enough to calm his baser instincts.

"Everything I know about you came from her letters. You understand that?"

"Yes. Do you have any with you?"

"Sorry. I don't. Actually I'm not sure I've even kept them back home."

"Where is home? In Vienna?"

"Oh, no. I live in Geneva and have for several years now. First in school and for the last six years at the United Nations."

"I didn't even know Heidi had a sister."

Brigid shrugs her shoulders.

"Maybe she didn't want you to know. Maybe she was afraid you might become interested in me."

Brigid smiles and allows the words to hover above them. She's using Heidi in some posthumous way to get even for an old injustice she is still unable to ignore or forgive. Nothing less. How ironic would it be if she were to steal Heidi's lover. But how, after all, does one steal the lover of someone who's already dead? Is it theft to steal property from someone who is no longer in a position to claim a loss? She still hates Heidi and always will, but she is not Heidi. She will not do what Heidi did. If she had wanted to be that way she would have tried to seduce Detective Wisdom. She almost did, but then caught herself in time. No, she's not Heidi, but the idea of a jealous Heidi pleases her immensely. At this thought her facial muscles surrender to an involuntary grin.

"You're smiling. Is something funny?"

"No. Sorry. I'm just thinking of the good times Heidi and I used to have."

He's silent, yet looks at her expectantly.

"Where shall I begin? You knew Heidi for over a year. Isn't that right?"

"Yes. Probably closer to two years since we first met."

"When did you meet exactly?"

"It was at one of the hospital Christmas parties. Two years this December."

"Then, right after the New Year started, she wrote to me about meeting a very extraordinary man. Your first name's Henry, isn't it?"

"Yes."

"Well, that makes you the one. She doesn't write that often, but whenever she does, you're mentioned. She tells me she loves you and always wants to be with you. I'm a little embarrassed to also say that she felt sex with you was like nothing she ever experienced before."

She stops talking and steals a look across the seat at him. A smile creeps across his face and she sees straight white teeth. He has not smiled before and it clearly enhances his looks. His eyes are closed now. Perhaps this little bit of lie is enough? Perhaps he is satisfied that Heidi and he are now joined in some kind of spiritual peace. His eyes open and he shakes his head as if to clear his vision.

"That woman at Posner's house who I stuck with the needle. It was an accident, you know. I tripped on the stairs. I never intended to hurt anyone. All I wanted to do was scare Posner into confessing. I never intended to hurt anyone. She's dead, isn't she? I saw the ambulance gurney leave the house. I was hiding down the street in an empty house. Then I followed you. But I didn't mean to hurt her. I didn't."

"I know you didn't and I'm sure the police know it as well."

He looks at her for a moment, his mouth partly open as if about to speak, then decides against talk and turns to gaze out the window. He turns back and sees her eyes quiver for a moment then close. A few seconds later she jumps awake.

"Sorry. I didn't mean to, well, you know, fall asleep."

"It's all right. You can sleep if you want. I won't hurt you. I promise, but then I need to look for where Heidi's buried and I want you to come with me. For now, rest a while. You're tired. We both are."

"Can I trust you?"

"Yes. Just rest. Rest. I'll be here."

She just closes her eyes without even repositioning herself or adjusting her clothing. In seconds a gentle snore fills the car. It has a relaxed rhythm, and in moments he feels like joining her, but he can't afford to. He reaches into his jacket and pulls out a small bottle. He uncaps it and draws out a few pills. He swallows them blindly and shakes his head. He's good for another six hours at least. That's enough. More than enough.

He replaces the bottle and feels the barrel of the pistol. He takes it out and lets it rest softly in his palm as if it were a small bird. What am I doing with this, he wonders? Or am I just going crazy? He holds it by the barrel and swings it in a tight arc behind him so he can position it beneath the back of the passenger seat.

She wakes after a several hours. An intense early afternoon sun fills the car, and in the warmth she shrugs out of a zippered cardigan. They are still parked in the small space behind a dumpster and between two shuttered motels. Henry stands a few feet beyond the car's hood and smokes. The more she studies his face without interruption, the more she's convinced he had no part in Heidi's disappearance. It is a gentle face. There is tenderness there that lies beneath his good looks. He also seems very troubled, and she can't help but wonder what Heidi made of that aspect of his personality.

She doesn't know about Posner. She's never even met him, doesn't even know what he looks like. From what Wisdom's told her, he wouldn't be a person they thought capable of such violence. She'd like to believe the story he told Henry, that Heidi's death was accidental and that Posner found and buried her out of panic. At this point though it doesn't matter anymore. She accepts that Heidi is dead. She wants to agree that it was an accident. She wants this all to be over and go back home to Switzerland and worry about Third World economics again. She doesn't want to see where Heidi is buried. She's sorry she can't feel grief, but that's it.

Stern turns and looks at her through the windshield. He tosses his cigarette away, moves a few steps, and reenters the car.

"I said you could rest. No one came. It's very quiet here. The season is long over. These motels are empty and most of the stores as well."

He slides into a sitting position behind the wheel, yawns deeply, and shakes his head once as if to clear away sleep, yet he seems very alert. He starts the engine and at first the noise seems deafening there in the quiet alley across from the beach. He lets it run for a few minutes, as if to awaken its six cylinders to join them for the final leg of the trip.

She looks at her watch. It's a little before two in the afternoon. She watches him drive with more restraint than he showed when they left the house that morning. The trip doesn't take long. They swing off the main road at a sign that announces the Montauk Overlook. He parks at the far end of the empty lot and cuts the engine just as he flips the trunk open with the inside handle. He slips out of the car and makes it obvious when he leaves the key in the ignition. It's a way of telling her that she can leave if she wants. Anytime she wants.

He moves to the trunk, reaches in, and comes away with a spade.

"I didn't have time to think of getting a proper shovel. It's the only thing I could find back in your house, but it should do. The ground here is very soft."

He goes back to close the trunk.

"Are you coming?"

"No. I accept that she's dead. That's all."

He doesn't speak, only turns and begins to walk into the cover of pine and cedar that extends outward from the parking lot before it dips down toward a beach. She looks around and sees why they call this place an overlook. From the car she has a clear view out to the northeast, all the way across a body of water to some distant low landmass that rises and falls out of a haze.

Her eyes follow him into the woods, but her view is clear. The sand pines and cedars are not thickly clustered, so she can follow him until he stops at a base of a misshapen sand pine shaped like the letter *L*. He rests one hand at the elbow of the bent tree, turns to face her, and then focuses his attention on the ground. He walks a few feet away, circles back around, stops, and begins to dig.

He works at it with intensity. Every few minutes he moves a few paces farther away from his last shallow trench. She wishes he would give it up, yet knows he won't. In less than ten minutes, he stops and bends down. He has found something. She knows. Just as he rises, she half turns her head in reaction to the grumble and screech of automobiles. She pivots in time to see two town police cars enter the lot in tandem. They are followed by two unmarked cars, one of which she recognizes as Wisdom's. They spread out across the empty parking area except for Wisdom's car, which heads straight for her. In seconds, a number of policemen are out and running across the lot toward the woods. Their pistols are drawn.

She turns her attention back to Stern who also hears the cars approach. He stands straight up and switches his hand grip around the spade as if to turn it into a club. He begins to wave it back and forth like a bat. She leaps from the car and begins to run toward him without stopping. From somewhere behind she hears Wisdom call her name.

"No. No, Henry. Put it down."

The words fly from her as she runs into the woods, but Henry doesn't seem to hear. He stands as before, holding the spade in two hands as the thought flashes through her that she has no idea whether he's defending himself or Heidi's grave.

# CHAPTER 29

At a quarter past two, Posner rides in a column of four cars that moves east from Montauk village. Two are unmarked sedans. All have overheads blinking into a bright early afternoon light. It doesn't take long for the convoy to reach a destination only a few miles east of the village. They slow and exit into the overlook before they fan out. If viewed from above, these maneuvers might look almost balletic.

The lot is empty except for a red Audi. Posner is in Bennett's car, which follows Wisdom's and parks in a spot parallel to, but twenty yards away, from the Audi. A woman with short dark hair is clearly visible in the passenger seat. Posner stays in Bennett's car with one officer. The plan is to bring him out as soon as the situation is secure. From the rear seat of the cruiser, Posner watches the exercise unfold. He can see it all. The woods seem far less overgrown than he remembers. Stern stands in front of the twisted tree; Posner's all too familiar grave site landmark. Stern's two hands grip what looks like a shovel, which he swings back and forth as if it were a baseball bat.

Four uniforms enter the woods from opposite sides and approach Stern in a pincer movement. Once in the woods they slow up, taking cautious steps around a range of scattered fallen branches and undergrowth while they keep their weapons pointed downward. In seconds they appear to be closing a circle around Stern.

The woman makes a sudden exit from the Audi and runs toward Stern shouting something. Posner imagines he recognizes a blurred facial resemblance to Heidi. She turns and moves away before he can get a better look, but he still feels an immediate fleeting angst that grabs his stomach muscles in a vise. Not possible, he mumbles to himself more than once. Not possible. He tells himself that whoever she is, she's not Heidi, and this process of rationalization begins to restore calm. With the windows closed, he only catches part of what she shouts, but the name "Henry" is unmistakably clear.

Wisdom runs behind the woman and calls out to her. Bennett trails Wisdom in a moderate jog. It's all a bit of a circus with everyone in motion.

Posner feels like everything that unfolds before him is in some bizarre way a tableau of his own creation; the phalanx of police cars, the officers converging on a lone man with their guns drawn, a woman he's never seen, two detectives he has, a wooded setting, and the man they're chasing. The poor dumb schmuck of a doctor doesn't have a chance. And all because Amos Posner either wasn't faithful enough to Sara by bringing the woman home in the first place, or wasn't unfaithful enough to have just fucked the woman and moved on. He has choreographed a disaster and is ordained to watch it all unfold.

And later he'll have to show them where to dig up Heidi's body. Where he told them he'd seen Stern. Almost where Stern now stands. The uniformed cop shifts to the right, opens the side widow and the drama now has full audio.

The woman shouts, "No. No, Henry. Put it down." The clarity almost shocks Posner, and he is unprepared for what happens next.

A thunderclap roars across the woods. The woman screams and falls forward as if pushed before disappearing beyond Posner's sight line. Just as she lands, Posner hears another loud crack and has his torso pushed into the seat cushion by his bodyguard cop.

"Down." The words are instinctive. Obedience is instant. Posner stays there with the officer's hands and chest pressed against his back.

They are so close he smells the faint soapy residue from the man's morning shower.

In what seems like minutes, although he later learns it was all over in less than sixty seconds, he is allowed to regain a sitting position. He sees Bennett approach his car. In the distance, a number of uniforms cluster around the area where he last saw Stern, but there is no sign of him. Another huddle of police stands near where he thought he last saw the woman fall. He sees Wisdom among them, obvious in his blue blazer and chinos, bending over some object on the ground. Less than ten minutes later an ambulance pulls into the lot and screeches to a stop beyond the Audi and blocks his further view. In moments, another appears as well and parks alongside the first.

There is a sense of controlled confusion as yet another two police cars arrive. Officers appear to mill around randomly, yet Posner suspects there is organization beyond the outward chaos.

Stern now appears as a vague shape at the very edge of Posner's view. He is surrounded by four officers as he moves into a police car, his wrists in cuffs.

"Bastard. Fucking bastard."

The words spew from Posner just as Bennett arrives at the car and opens the rear door.

"Time to put an end to all of this. Are you up to it?" He seems unduly solicitous considering all the trouble Posner's put him through. At that moment another wave of grief attempts to overwhelm him. Somehow Bennett senses this and hugs him. Just like that. A hug a big brother might give him. Bennett is anything but the dashing television image of a policeman. Posner returns the hug. Now he's ready to go ahead.

He exits the car, and they begin to walk into the woods.

"What happened there? I heard what sounded like a shot. Maybe more than one."

"Later," is all Bennett says.

From the corner of his eye, Posner sees a gurney being loaded into one of the ambulances. Wisdom is there and closes the rear door. Then a quick wave and the driver takes off for the trip to Southampton Hospital.

"Who was that?"

"I said later. Just keep going. We're almost there."

Posner's eyes focus on the area directly ahead. A truncated focal length creates a kind of tunnel vision. All he sees is the gnarled sand pine looming ahead surrounded by a small cluster of uniformed police. When he's within fifteen feet of the area, he notices two white-coated medical personnel and behind them an empty stretcher that rests on a gurney. He comes to a stop outside the circle of police and signals to Bennett. He stretches an arm outright towards spot on the ground that is already disturbed with the removal of a few shovelfuls of sandy soil. He sees a piece of silver plastic sticking out, nearly upright, like a marker mountain climbers leave.

"Here," he says in a weak voice that follows his outstretched arm. "Right here."

It's all there. Nothing's changed. So close to the surface Posner wonders how it ever survived undisturbed for all these months despite weather, animals, or even the occasional hiker. He's positioned about ten feet away and watches two policemen with shovels move the soft soil from around the silver plastic. A form becomes more obvious as the surface material is removed. A departmental photographer's camera clicks a procession of digital images.

Someone bends down and makes a small cut across the plastic. From his position he clearly sees the front of one white shoe stick out. He remembers the painted toenails and wants to be sick. He turns away just as Bennett joins him and supports an elbow.

"I think we have enough for now. Let's take you back. First to headquarters and then where? Back to the hospital?"

"I guess so. At least for tonight."

Bennett waves a patrolman closer and arranges for Posner to be returned to the county patrol car. Posner blindly walks in front of the policeman, his face a mask of sheer granite.

He sits alone in the car. The patrolman stands outside and speaks quietly into a handheld radio. Every few minutes the cop signs off and takes some nibble from an inside jacket pocket to chew. Posner needs to sleep. He knows it, but he is afraid of the dreams. Peace has its own price, but he doubts he will ever again find such comfort.

Bennett returns thirty minutes later. He enters the car and sits next to Posner. Two uniforms sit in front and one starts the engine and pulls out of the parking area as other vehicles still enter. He sees Posner watch the flow of traffic.

"They'll be at it for quite a while yet."

Posner feels insane, yet despite Sara's death he senses a burden lifting.

Bennett leans back, pulls a small notebook from his jacket pocket and scratches something in the book with a fat ballpoint pen that was clipped to the edge. He finishes and notices Posner's gaze as he returns the book to his jacket. He holds up the fat stubby ballpoint.

"I get them at the place where I have my stuff dry-cleaned. First pen I ever had that has a clip wide enough to fit around the notepad and not get lost. Isn't that something?"

Posner smiles at the folksy way Bennett has let him enter his personal life. He doesn't ask if Bennett has a family, yet assumes he must. Posner then becomes aware that he's smiling. He leans back into the seat and sleeps, but there are no dreams.

He wakes to the muted sound of Bennett on his cell phone. Bennett looks at him and snaps the phone shut with one hand. Posner looks out the window and sees they are nearly in East Hampton. He couldn't have dozed for long. His right arm rests just beneath the window, the hospital plastic identification tag still around his wrist. He reads his name and date of birth on the narrow plastic strip. There is also an unknown doctor's name. He remembers nothing of his hospital admittance. He wishes he could forget that day on the Jitney just as easily, yet knows he never will.

"Feel better?"

"Yes. Thank you."

"Good then. Let me fill you in on what's happened. First, the body is that of Heidi Kashani. We won't have official confirmation till the County ME's office runs fingerprint and dental checks, but certain things in the field gave us good prelim results, like the pink-and-white dress. There was also the ID in her bag that was buried with her."

Posner listens, but says nothing at first. All he can think of is sliding the straw bag across her body and into the plastic. And then out again to get the cell phone. And how lucky he was to have worn gloves and not leave prints. He shivers at the memory, and then speaks to quiet the images.

"What happened back there?"

"You did hear shots, two of them in fact. One of the troopers tripped over a log and discharged his weapon by accident into the ground. Another was so trigger-happy that the first round spooked him into doing the same thing. Lucky both shells hit nothing but dirt."

"So no one was hurt?"

"Not exactly. The woman you probably saw is Heidi's sister from Europe. She got scared by the gunshots, tripped over something and took a bad fall."

"I saw her falling forward."

"Well, she seems okay except for a probable broken bone in her foot, but nothing more than that beyond some facial scratches from the underbrush."

"No one ever said she had a sister."

"She looks a lot like Heidi. It was going to be a surprise, but things got out of hand before we could drop the bombshell on you and Stern."

"On me?"

"It was a long shot, but you were one of the early suspects. Sorry."

Posner exhales slowly before he looks straight up and into Bennett's eyes.

"I think I understand. What happened to him? To Stern?"

He almost spits the name out.

"Our troopers were surrounding him. He was standing near the grave site holding a shovel as a weapon."

"I saw that from the car."

"When the gunshots went off and Brigid fell, he dropped the shovel and went to her. Must have thought she'd been hit. Damnedest thing I ever saw. A day before he kidnaps her and does God knows what else, and then he drops his only weapon and runs out to help her. We took him in without a struggle. All he cared about was whether she was all right."

"What about the gun? The one he took from my house."

"Funny guy, the doctor. He disarmed himself long before they got to the woods. It was under the back of the passenger seat in her Audi all the time he was out there with only a shovel, or a spade, if you want to be technical."

Posner starts to speak, his mouth half open, and then stops. Some remote part of his conscience wants him to say that he could see Stern never intended to kill Sara. That it was all an accident. That Stern was holding the needle and was running out when he tripped on the stairs and fell into her. And that everything that happened to both Heidi and Sara was somehow all his fault. But he says nothing. It's easier to blame Stern for everything. Nothing he could say will bring Sara back.

"Want to say something?"

When Posner doesn't answer, Bennett arches an eyebrow, looks away, and shakes his head. He also says nothing and tilts his head toward the window to stare at the passing village landscape and avoid further eye contact.

Posner takes in all of this. Bennett is probably thinking what a poor bastard I am. And that neither I nor Stern deserved any of this, but that's the way things sometimes work out.

He watches the light dim as evening crawls in. Another five minutes till they get to headquarters. Another five minutes till he'll need to face Bennett and the others and the whole process again. This time with the County people. After that it'll all be over and back to the hospital. He shuts his eyes. He no longer needs the rest, but he'd rather not speak.

# CHAPTER 30

Wisdom notes the time in his appointment book and circles it. The call came from the Austrian Consulate in Manhattan. They'll be picking Brigid Kashani up the following day and taking her to JFK for an early evening flight to Geneva. Will he have time to see her on her way to the airport? At about two in the afternoon? She would like to say goodbye and thank him in person. Their language is all very formal and he feels his positive reply was equally proper.

As the time approaches to see Brigid, he can't avoid having his thoughts drawn back to the case. It isn't hard. Only ten days have gone by since the events at the Montauk Overlook. Dr. Henry Stern is undergoing psychiatric evaluation at Stony Brook Hospital Medical Center. He will likely be there for some time. The county attorney suggests that Stern will face a bevy of charges ranging from unlawful entry, auto theft, assault, battery, sexual abuse, and kidnapping relating to Brigid, and either manslaughter or murder two with regard to Sara Posner. They are still collecting evidence regarding his involvement in the death of Heidi Kashani, but murder charges are also likely in that case. Amos Posner's observation of him at the burial site is compelling evidence together with Stern's lack of alibi on the day she disappeared. And Stern's countercharges against Posner sound no more than the incoherent ramblings of a cornered unstable man.

Amos Posner has been cleared of any involvement in Heidi's death. It was never an issue. Wisdom spoke to Posner on the phone the previous day. While still distraught, he seems to be regaining some sense of emotional control. He projects guilt about the loss of his wife that initially puzzles Wisdom, until he realizes he knows nothing of their relationship and its hidden crevices. Posner did seem genuinely pleased when Wisdom tells him that both he and Bennett will be at the forthcoming funeral service, which can now occur with the release of his wife's body.

Posner says he plans on selling the house as soon as possible and will, at some future date, be moving to northern California, as he and his wife had planned. Tomorrow he plans to come back to Amagansett from the city, where he's been living, to go through his personal items. It is not a task Wisdom envies. Posner babbles on randomly for several minutes, but Wisdom lets him speak without interruption. At one point, Posner breaks into what Wisdom would only later describe as an ironic laugh, when he says he has heard from his lawyer that the Justice Department is dropping all of its inquiries into some past activities. Referring to his lawyer's call, Posner keeps repeating the phrase, "This means I'm innocent," over and over. Wisdom later thinks Posner might have referred to more than his federal issues, but he will never be sure. In retrospect Posner almost reminds him of one of those tragic figures in literature he studied in college. The poor son of a bitch inadvertently created his own mess by the simple act of speaking to a woman on a public bus. Unbelievable!

At three minutes to the hour his phone rings. Herr Weis calls from the car that they are there and parked outside headquarters.

"I'll be right out," Wisdom replies.

He would not think of having Brigid try to walk one extra step with a broken bone in her foot. The fall she took at the overlook could have done more damage, but she will still need a cast and crutches for another month at least. On the phone he's tried to persuade her to stay on here to recuperate, but his suggestion was, at best, half-hearted. He knows she'll never be able to fully relax as long as she wakes every morning to the sights and smells of the same air her sister breathed before she died, to say nothing of what she herself has gone through. She has given all the necessary depositions. She might be recalled for a trial, but the county attorney doubts it will be necessary. She dismisses the fact that she has a little time left on her lease.

No. It's best for her to be on her way. It's also best for him. He admits he went through a period of temptation that tested his own fidelity, or innocence in a way. He passed it once, but admits that he doesn't fully trust himself to keep passing. No. Best that she doesn't stay.

The car is a black Mercedes limo. How opulent, he thinks as he approaches, then mentally reprimands himself. She does have a broken foot and the limo has far more leg room.

Within her diplomatic community, she has also become somewhat of a celebrity. Weis approaches and extends a hand. Wisdom takes it and can't help noticing that Weis wears a suit conspicuously like the one he wore at their first meeting a few months ago; a dark well-tailored charcoal-gray with a creamy white shirt and a matching dark tie. His shoes are polished black and shine like new glass. Maybe the man only has one set of clothes he thinks and smiles at the absurdity of the idea. Weis just seems to accept the smile as an example of traditional American friendliness.

"The driver and I will be over there," Weis says pointing to a spot some fifty feet away.

The air is cool, but the sun pours enough heat through a clear sky, so neither Weis nor his driver need coats.

As Wisdom nears the car he sees that the rear limo door is slightly ajar. He pulls it fully open. She's leaning back on one end of the seat with one leg propped across its length. A small cast encases her foot. She's dressed much like when they first met, a dark suit jacket with matching pants and a simple white blouse buttoned to the neck. He notices and compliments her on a cameo pin that rests on her jacket lapel.

"Oh. This is new. I bought it at a shop in Sag Harbor yesterday. One good thing to remind me of this trip, excluding you and your colleagues, of course."

Wisdom notices she emphasizes *you* and smiles.

"Please step in, if you don't mind. There's room to sit on your end of the seat."

"Thank you." He moves in and sits while avoiding the crutches on the floor.

"How's the foot?"

"Getting better. I shouldn't have too much problem after a few more weeks."

"You must be happy to be going back home."

"Well, I'm happy that all this is over and we know what happened to Heidi. I'm sorry this mess cost the life of Mr. Posner's wife and basically destroyed his life and that of Dr. Stern."

"You were very brave when it came to Stern."

"Not really. Maybe at first, but then I realized he was no more than a frightened young man. Once that sunk in, I no longer felt in danger. Will he go to prison?"

Wisdom tries to avoid any opinion, however obvious the answer might be. It's the way he was trained.

"That depends on all of his psychiatric exams, but I'd say that one way or another he'll be incarcerated for some time."

"He didn't really want to kill anyone, you know. It was all what the English call 'bluster.'"

"That may be true. Someday, maybe a jury will decide." As he speaks he realizes she's only thinking about Sara Posner, and not her sister.

"If there's ever a trial, I'd like to come back and speak in his defense."

"But he kidnapped you. Then threatened to rape and kill you."

"But he didn't. That's the important thing. Don't you think?"

Wisdom doesn't answer. He has no answer. The question is too moral in these circumstances and certainly too bizarre. All he can do is shrug his shoulders. Stern is a man who kidnapped and threatened a woman, most probably killed her sister, and then killed an innocent woman bystander and who now gains sympathy from the kidnap victim. No. He has no answer that makes any sense.

"Will you tell your parents?"

"No. It will only cause confusion and more grief. For them she died some time ago. It's best to leave it that way."

That's when he tells her about his conversation with the rabbi in Brooklyn and Heidi's volunteer work. He can't let that bit of insight stay hidden. Brigid shakes her head in wonderment, yet says nothing at first.

"Maybe she was trying to somehow redeem herself," adds Wisdom, who's still not sure whether raising the issue is worth it.

"Perhaps you're right, but there could be other reasons as well. For my family and me it's still too little and too late as you say here. Still, thank you for telling me. Maybe some part of Heidi was better than we ever thought. I hope so."

For a moment Wisdom thinks she might cry, but Brigid is tough to the end. Maybe in private, he thinks, but not in front of another person, especially a man. There doesn't seem much more to say. She beckons him to come closer, then leans forward, kisses him on the cheek, and makes it seems like the most natural thing in the world. Her mouth lingers for a fraction long enough for him to inhale some scent. Then she pulls back.

"Go home and take care of your wife and children."

He has only the one son, but doesn't correct her. He smiles at the thought that with woman's intuition maybe she knows more than he does.

"Is something funny?"

"No. I'm just happy you don't blame me for putting you in possible danger."

"You did no such thing."

But he did screw up and no amount of sugarcoating can hide it. He knows he'll just have to live with it all and move on. He starts to step back into the street, but holds onto the top of the open door with one hand.

"Goodbye then. Safe flight."

"Goodbye to you, Peter. Oh, I forgot something."

She turns around to reach behind her and with a small effort pulls an object closer before she hands it to him.

"It seems foolish to just throw it out. Your people were very nice and gave it back to me. After all, it did cost well over a hundred dollars. Perhaps you can give it to someone to use. I've even had it cleaned."

Her arm swings forward and passes him the top of a metal hanger that supports a clear plastic dry cleaning bag. The pink-and-white pattern is plainly visible. He takes the bag and in the transfer process feels a fleeting touch of her fingers. He steps all the way out of the car, turns and waves to Weis who has seen his movement and is already walking toward the car with the uniformed driver in tow. They shake hands again. He waves at the rear of the black car as it moves out of the lot, and notes with mixed emotions that Brigid doesn't look back.

At the automatic glass door entrance to headquarters he realizes that he's still holding a metal hanger with a clean, almost new pink-and-white dress. He stares at the dress for a moment and wonders how such a seemingly insignificant garment could have in its own way propagated the death of two people and ruined the lives of two others. He looks around, a combination of indecision and embarrassment, and then drops the garment in the metal wastebasket to the right of the automatic doors. It will sit undisturbed among the used coffee cups, food wrappers, and other assorted garbage that visitors and cops both leave there until the next day's pickup.

He nods to the desk officer, walks through the side door to his cubicle, and punches in his home number. Maybe they could all go out for pizza tonight.

# CHAPTER 31

Posner enters the house for what he imagines will be the last time. It's his first trip back without the police since Sara died. He unlocks and pushes open the front door and half expects a weight to impede its progress. Yet the door has no memory and glides open smoothly, as if Heidi's body had never blocked its movement. He steps into the hall and for a moment stands where Sara died in his arms. He cannot stop the tears that come and doesn't try. The impossibility of the two separate deaths within almost the same space overwhelms him. He hesitates in the doorway as he regains some control, while he burns with anger first at Stern and then at himself.

Others are waiting behind him, but they are patient and say nothing. They all know what he's been through. He's listed his home with a local broker. There are two movers with him and someone who calls herself a relocation consultant. He needs the help. They will go through everything he owns and segregate items either for disposal, contribution, sale, or storage pending ultimate shipment to the West Coast. For now he still sleeps in the New York apartment, but he's also put that up for sale. He tries to think of other things. Nothing will bring Sara back. He lives with his own guilt.

He needs to move far away and plans to make a deposit on a two-bedroom house rental in Napa Valley. From the photos the house seems small, which is what he wants. It sits on a third of an elevated acre, but the adjacent house has at least ten acres of planted grape vines that roll up the hill toward him. An option to buy is included in the lease. The purchase price seems very high, although he understands that Napa seems to have inflated real estate values. He is now prepared to spend his days looking at sunsets over a vineyard instead of sunrises over the ocean.

The important thing now is to get away. He spends the next two hours supervising what to do with furniture, paintings, lithographs, file cabinets, and an assorted medley of things he's kept without purpose. He's long since disposed of the windbreaker and its content of broken heel and bit of plastic. Satisfied with their progress, he leaves the others to their tasks, retreats to the master bedroom, and closes the door. He tosses a suitcase on the bed and fills it with those items of his clothing he wishes to keep. The rest he consigns to a large plastic bag for delivery to a local nonprofit, or into another trash bag to be tossed. He fills a separate bag with Sara's things, first from the closet and then out of the undersized dresser. She never kept too much clothing here. It might make too much of a commitment.

In her second dresser drawer he swallows a deep breath as he pulls out a few worn pages from a dated woman's magazine wedged behind two sweaters. The article seems to be a brief guide to enhancing prospects for pregnancy. He notes it begins with a discussion of ovulation cycles and the heading immediately ratchets his memory back several years.

He repeats the same thought he's had since his legal troubles began that everything might have been very different if there were children. He might have shifted his workload, or more importantly, his work ethic, so he could spend more time at home. There would never have been a Heidi or a Stern. He still thinks of this, years after he and Sara have stopped trying to get pregnant. Yes. Things would have been very different if there were children. He crumples the pages into a tight wad and flings them into the bag of trash.

The last item from a side drawer is a black tee shirt. He holds it in his hands before he buries his face in the cotton. The cloth mutes his sobs so those in the next room cannot hear. He staggers backward until his legs reach the bed. He sits and blames himself over and over, but there is nothing more to do.

Stern is now under observation in a psychiatric ward. There is no question of his guilt in Sara's death. Wisdom and Bennett have both told him that if a person introduces a lethal weapon to a scene, then the person is guilty of a crime, probably manslaughter, even if the ensuing death was accidental.

Stern will also likely be convicted of Heidi's death, despite the man's denial of guilt and attempts to implicate Posner. The theory seems clear. Jealousy must have possessed him to follow the bus in a rented car and then trail the two of them through their tour of the area and then to Posner's house. While he was out searching for his wallet, Stern came in and confronted Heidi. He either pushed her or she fell to her death. Everything after that just added to his need to protect himself. His report of her disappearance, the visit to the local police, and even his visit to Posner were all meant to draw suspicion away from himself.

The only dicey part was the burial. At first, Stern must have gone nuts wondering why her death wasn't reported. Indeed, he did follow Posner out to the overlook and that's what he'd told the cops. Still, it was his word against Posner's, and Stern was the one with both the motive and opportunity. And besides, anyone involved can see the man's a nutcase. Posner is blameless with regard to Heidi's death according to the County District Attorney's Office. He has no intention of ever admitting to the burial. What good would it possibly do? He has even researched the penalties for unlawful disposal of a body and they are relatively minor. No. He will not involve himself in the burial. He is now free to move to the coast whenever he wants, as long as he makes himself available, if necessary, for a trial.

He seethes with hate whenever he thinks of Stern. The man will get what he deserves, but it will not bring Sara back. Dammit! He thought things were going to be better after that weekend in the city. And then everything fell apart. Like Humpty Dumpty. Except that no one can put his life together again. He wipes his face with her shirt, holds it to his cheek, and then slips it into the bag with the rest of her clothes.

He's gone through everything except for the white leather jewelry box on the dresser. He remembers she only kept costume stuff in this house. She either wore her engagement and wedding rings, or kept them in the apartment with other items like the Mikimoto pearls and the jade pendant he'd bought for her in Taiwan. He sighs, pulls the box off the dresser, and sits back down on the bed.

There isn't much to go through. Certainly nothing of value. It's much more a sort of junk container than a jewelry box. He finds a broken Swatch watch, a "Kerry '04" button, and three boxes of matches from The Lodge restaurant in East Hampton crammed under schedules for a local yoga studio and the Hampton Jitney. He reaches for the trash bag and begins to drop in the junk items. There is no jewelry and so he decides to toss the box away as well. When he lifts it though, he hears a small rattle. He reopens the box and sees a part of a gold chain wedged in the back of the lower shelf. A slight pull and it springs free. It is a thin gold chain necklace from which hangs a small capital *H*.

He freezes. The chain drops to the carpet, but his hands cannot move. There is no question where it came from. His image of Heidi is real. She stands near the stairs and fingers the necklace while she tells him it was a gift from Stern. He sees her chest heave and her lips swell and part. It's all so real.

"Ahhhh!" The sound flies wildly from his mouth.

"You okay in there?" One of the movers asks. He mumbles an answer.

"Yes. Okay." That's all he can summon.

He reaches down and lifts the necklace. He fondles the *H* as Heidi once did. A deep breath barely helps, but the hammering in his heart eases. He closes his eyes.

"You were here, weren't you?"

He speaks as if Sara is still in the room. Putting away laundry or combing her hair in front of the dresser mirror.

"It wasn't Stern. It was you. You came home early. While I was out looking for my wallet. Maybe you were planning to get here early all along to check out whether I was with someone. Maybe there never was a meeting with a client here on Long Island, but you did have a rented car. That's how you got here. And when you found her here you thought you were right all along, didn't you? Thought I was screwing someone while you were in the city."

He stops and opens his eyes, but she's not there. He can't explain. She can't explain. He closes his eyes again.

"Did you fight? Did you push her? Maybe she started to fall and you reached out to help.

"Maybe you grabbed onto the necklace and it came away as she fell."

He unclasps his hand and looks down. The chain is broken in the rear clasp where it was torn from her neck.

"I can see it."

And for a moment he can. He watches as Heidi falls down the stairs in a grotesque dive as death swallows her scream.

"You tried to save her and she fell away. Right away you thought she was dead so you left. Maybe you didn't even know you were holding the necklace until you'd driven off. Is that how it happened? Answer me, dammit! And when were you going to say something? Were you waiting for the cops to come calling? Or were waiting for me to confess it all? That we had a thing going, but I never did because nothing ever happened. Nothing."

His eyes begin to glisten. He turns his head and looks through the bedroom window, but the view is limited to the oldest house on the block, a weather-beaten cottage across the street on nearly an acre. There is no ocean view out there to lose himself in while he tries to make sense of it all.

"But she might also have fallen while I was out and before you came home. I mean the stairs were newly refinished, weren't they?"

The thought brings him a moment's reprieve from his first instinct, but the idea loses steam almost as quickly.

"If that's what happened, then why would you take the necklace if you came in and found Heidi dead? No way. And even if you thought I'd killed her and then gone out for something to help cover it up, you never would have just bent over and pulled the necklace away. No. You had to have struggled. That's the only way it could have happened."

A knock on the door brings him back.

"Mr. Posner."

Another knock.

"Mr. Posner. You all right?"

"Yeah."

"We're almost finished out here. Anything else that needs to be done before we get to the bedroom?"

Posner cannot speak.

"Sir. Anything else?"

"Just one thing. I'll be a minute."

Footsteps move away from the door. Posner stands and walks around to the other side of the bed. He looks down at the night table, on which rests a lamp, clock radio, and phone. One hand still grasps the necklace. He spreads the necklace out on the table and smoothes out the chain.

"And the night just after it happened. The night I planned to meet you at the airport and you cancelled and said we needed a separation. I thought it was just more of your growing jealousy and looking for you in the terminal, I couldn't think of anything else. It all made a kind of mad sense at the time. Your suspicions had been developing for months. And when you saw Heidi at the house, it all came together. You thought you knew it all about Heidi and me. And you never let on. Not a word. So we spent all those days and nights afterwards either not speaking at all, or when we did, never daring to share our secrets. God, you must have hated me then, yet somehow time allowed you to change enough to forgive me in spite of everything you thought I did. Maybe you forgave me because it was the only way you could forgive yourself for what happened to Heidi."

He blinks his eyes a few times, but there are no more tears.

"Just one thing," he repeats to the empty room, but it's not really empty. Sara's here.

Wherever he looks she's here.

He pulls out his wallet and fishes out a card. He sits on the bed, picks up the phone, and punches in Peter Wisdom's direct line.